"Megan, get moving away from here."

"Not without you." She took a step toward him, the flashlight on her phone a bright eye in the darkness around her. "I'm not leaving—"

"It's a trap," he shouted.

He didn't know how or where; he just knew no one left the door open with a dead body inside without a truly good reason. Trapping two people he had already tried to kill would be a truly good reason to the killer of the woman inside.

Jack kept backing away, his gaze on the body, the table, the doorway. He saw no wires to indicate an explosive, no movement to indicate a shooter taking aim. The area was shockingly silent, so silent his footfalls on the deck planks sounded like thunder, like branches creaking in a high wind.

No, not his footfalls. The branches were creaking, casting shadows in the light from the house and his phone flashlight. Yet the night was still silent.

"Jack, run," Megan cried. "The tree—"

A thunderous roar drowned out Megan's scream.

Laurie Alice Eakes dreamed of being a writer from the time she was a small child. Now, with her dreams fulfilled, she is the award-winning and bestselling author of over two dozen historical and contemporary novels. When she isn't writing full-time, she enjoys long walks, live theater and being near her beloved Lake Michigan. She lives in Illinois with her husband and sundry cats and dogs.

Books by Laurie Alice Eakes

Love Inspired Suspense

Perilous Christmas Reunion
Lethal Ransom
Exposing a Killer

Visit the Author Profile page at Harlequin.com.

EXPOSING A KILLER

LAURIE ALICE EAKES

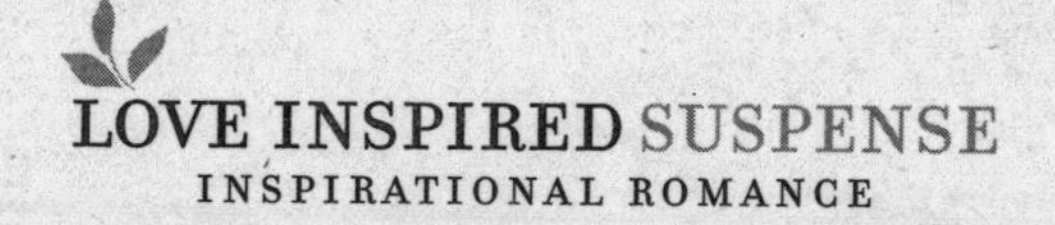

ISBN-13: 978-1-335-55448-2

Exposing a Killer

This edition published by arrangement with Harlequin Books S.A.

For questions and comments about the quality of this book, please contact us at CustomerService@Harlequin.com.

Love Inspired
22 Adelaide St. West, 40th Floor
Toronto, Ontario M5H 4E3, Canada
www.Harlequin.com

Printed in U.S.A.

Thou art my hiding place; thou shalt preserve me from trouble; thou shalt compass me about with songs of deliverance. Selah.

—*Psalms* 32:7

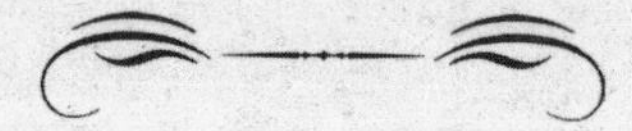

To Sharon, Patricia and Sherrill.
Thank you for not giving up on me
over the past couple of years of my erratic creativity.
Your support has kept me going with my writing.

ONE

The voices rasped through the night too low for Megan O'Clare to hear, but their tone sliced the near darkness sharper than a butcher's knife. Two voices. Male. Female. Through her binoculars, Megan could only see the male. His broad shoulders blocked the woman from view, towering over her, his hands raised as though he gripped her shoulders.

At least Megan hoped he held her shoulders and not the woman's neck. The growling of his muted words suggested the latter was not at all out of the realm of possibilities.

Megan shivered on the branch of an overgrown oak, where she had taken up her observation point. Not on the property of her subject, the unseen woman. That would have been trespassing, a no-no, especially for a private investigator like Megan. But she was as close to the couple as she dared get in the branches of a tree that leaned over the backyard fence of the house next door, a house from which she had watched a throng of college students swarm toward food and entertainment elsewhere. Not one had thought to leave an outside light on, for which Megan was grateful. Her subject, Elizabeth Cahill, and her male companion had shared their company under fairy lights strung along the railings of the deck.

The night had started out romantic, giving Megan a twinge of guilt for spying on them, however legitimate her reason for doing so. Or maybe a twinge of envy that she was sitting in a tree observing them dine and dance, while she worked on bringing this case to a close instead of enjoying someone's company on a Friday night.

At least she *had* nudged shoulders with the green-eyed monster until the argument began.

If only she owned a device that brought conversations as close to her ears as her binoculars brought scenes to her eyes. Then she could understand the argument rather than guessing at its content.

Cahill shouldn't have been able to dance. The man shouldn't have drawn her into the motion. She was supposed to be suffering from an injured back after slipping and falling on a wet floor at work. Cahill's employer suspected the woman was malingering and had hired Megan to investigate. A week of failing to find any evidence of workmen's compensation fraud during the day had driven Megan into the tree on a Friday night.

At least the sacrifice of forgoing a silly movie and popcorn with her roommate had paid off—literally. She'd managed to video the woman dancing with grace and ease, and she kept the recording rolling as the argument escalated, the man's grumble turning into a growl like a dog preparing to attack.

Megan leaned forward, and the branch creaked beneath her. In the quiet of neighborhood, the sound reverberated.

The voices ceased. The man glanced around. For the first time that night, Megan saw his face clearly, lit by a nearby fairy light. His mustache and beard were reddish, more auburn than Megan's own copper ponytail, his hair trimmed and darker. He had bushy eyebrows, a large, well-shaped nose and eyes, almost too big for good proportion to his other features, even the nose.

And another chill ran down Megan's spine despite the moderate temperature of the autumn night. She doubted he could see her. He was in little light. She was in less. Her clothes were dark, and she had pulled the hood of her sweatshirt over her red hair. Dangling leaves shielded the pale skin of her face. Yet eyes like those surely saw… too much.

The tree rustled around Megan. She couldn't feel it, but the wind must have picked up. Maybe the man would blame the creaking branch on the breeze.

She snapped a still shot of his face as the video kept rolling, knowing the image would be dark without the flash, but hoping she got something to identify him should she need a witness later for Cahill's employer.

Rather than turning back to his argument, the man stepped away and strode to the rail of the deck. His hands curled around the wood, and his body bent forward as though he struggled to catch his breath.

Behind him, the woman lay in a crumpled heap against the house wall like a discarded bundle of rags.

Megan's heart squeezed into her stomach. She swallowed hard to keep the "No, no, no, no" from pouring across her lips.

Not dead. Not dead. The woman could not be—

A hand clamped on her shoulder. Megan jumped. She flung up her right hand to defend herself from attack and lost her grip. She began to slide toward the end of the branch. It bowed and creaked beneath her, then snapped like a gunshot, and Megan tumbled to the ground. To mercifully soft grass. Still, she made a thud loud enough to be heard from her position in the Lincoln Park neighborhood to the Southside neighborhood of Hyde Park ten miles away. The impact drove the wind from her lungs, immobilizing her.

"You can't stay there." A murmuring voice close at hand—close enough for Megan to hear without a special device.

Breath catching in her lungs again, she managed to look up at the tall, broad figure against the ambient light of a city at night. Spots danced before her eyes. She needed to scramble to her feet, needed to run. Her simple investigation had just turned somewhere between scary and deadly. Too close to deadly.

"Let's go before he sees us." The man bent and grabbed her hand.

But *he* had already seen them. A blaze of light stabbed the dimness of the yards and a crack followed. Not a breaking limb this time. Not the backfiring car or slamming door she wished for.

A gunshot.

She started to drop to the ground to roll into a fetal position against the base of the tree.

"Run." The stranger clasped her hand.

Megan jerked away from him. "Don't touch me."

"Go."

A second explosion gave her the impetus she needed to apply her running shoes for what they were intended. Her high school track coach had never seen her sprint as she did with gunfire coming closer. Not fast enough. No one ran faster than a bullet, but she gave it a try. If only she were taller, had longer legs like the stranger keeping pace beside her.

Keeping pace. With his height, he should have long left her behind.

The shooter had long legs, too, and wasn't slowing his

stride to match a woman of medium height. He gained on them yard by yard.

Megan ducked between two cars parked on the curb and raced across the quiet street—a street quiet enough someone was sure to call the cops any moment. But any moment might be too late.

She sought an opening between cars again. Trees shadowed the block from the streetlights. In her dark hoodie and jeans, she would be harder to see, though her pounding feet sounded like amplified bass drumbeats. Her heart raced twice as fast and just as loudly. Her breath snagged in her throat, each inhalation whooping. She needed to up her exercise game. She would start tomorrow.

If she survived tonight.

No openings between cars. She leaped onto the hood of something low and sporty and rolled to the other side, landing on all fours on the parkway.

"Nice move." The stranger landed beside her on his feet, as light as a cat, then dropped to a crouch beside her, his hand on her shoulder. "Stay down."

"My car's on the next—"

A gentle finger touched her lips in a warning to remain quiet. Her lips tingled. She caught her breath, inhaling his scent of plain soap and clothes hung in the sun to dry.

And she heard the crackle of a footfall slipping over dried leaves. Once. Twice. Stealthy steps, not a casual stroller.

Though her breathing had slowed to normal in the momentary respite, Megan's heart began to race again.

Across the street, the snick of someone chambering a round bounced between brick buildings as though he had lobbed a super ball instead of prepared his weapon.

If only it were a high-velocity rubber ball and not a bullet about to soar their way.

But the shot never came. The footfalls receded with the squeak of a sole on blacktop, the swish of fabric, a lessening of pressure in the finger still sealing her lips.

"Let's go," her companion began.

Megan was already on her feet, running from the gunman, running from the strange sensation still buzzing through her lips. If she could reach the alley, her car wasn't far from the other end.

That was a big if.

"Where?" the stranger asked.

Where what?

She didn't answer. She needed her breath for running. The shots had ceased. The shooter was bound to hear them and turn around. Maybe he already had. Over the thud, thud, thud of her footfalls and the stranger's against the uneven concrete sidewalk, she could hear nothing else. Tree roots and winter's freezes and thaws over the years had shoved the slabs of the sidewalk up and down like miniature hills complete with ledges just high enough to catch a toe and send a body flying face-first onto the unyielding ground.

She didn't like the idea that a person who had shot at her no doubt still lurked somewhere on the street. Rows of town houses and multiplex apartment buildings offered no form of refuge. She must reach her car, drive into a commercial district. Only two blocks away. But it felt like a marathon, with a gunman on the loose with her in his sights.

Was the stranger at her side involved? Possible. He appeared, and the shooting began. Or they both might have simply been caught in the crosshairs of someone else's trouble. They were witnesses to a possible murder, which was enough for the killer to want them dead next.

She was ready to collapse. All Chicago blocks were

one eighth of a mile, her aunt Sally always told her. This one was surely eight miles long.

She stumbled on a missing piece of concrete and grabbed a utility pole for support.

"All right?" the stranger asked.

"I'd be more all right if you weren't here drawing fire."

Perhaps unfair. Perhaps he didn't deserve the suggested accusation.

He didn't deny it. He merely passed her with one lengthy stride and turned to his right, then stopped. They had reached the alley. He must be looking for pursuit.

Megan didn't wait to find out what he saw. She swerved left and sped down the alley. At least dumpsters allowed a modicum of shelter if the gunman came after her again.

Someone came after her. The alley gravel crunched under rubber soles. Megan dove for the nearest dumpster.

"It's me." The strange man again.

Like his presence should be reassuring.

With the reek of used kitty litter in her nose from the bin she'd nearly used for shelter, she chose to keep going. Ten yards. Six. Two. Her nondescript sedan crouched against the curb. She shoved her hand into her pocket and clicked the lock release. The chirp reassured her. Though she had no reason to fear it, she never discounted the possibility of a dead battery in a moment of crisis.

She yanked the door open with one hand and shoved the key into the ignition with the other before she fully settled in her seat. She released the parking brake and stepped on the gas, steering one-handed while she yanked her door shut. She barely missed the bumper of a minivan, then a *thunk* warned her she might have clipped the fender of a car across the road. She glanced to her right and realized the thunk came from the passenger-side door.

She wasn't alone in her car.

* * *

Jack Luskie thought his chances with the gunman might be better than with Megan O'Clare, who was a private investigator with Gary Flanagan Investigations, as her boss, Gary, had informed Jack when they'd spoken of the Cahill case. Her driving was erratic. Then again, she was frightened by the gunshots and probably by him. He probably shouldn't have gotten into her car without asking first, but he didn't have wheeled transportation for a quick getaway. He had taken the L to the town house of Cahill, a woman he needed to catch embezzling from her company if he wanted to be paid.

Of course he wanted to be paid. He needed the income.

He didn't need to end up smashed against a telephone pole. One loomed terrifyingly close to the front bumper of the woman's vehicle. He started to shout a warning, then realized if she couldn't see the danger, they were doomed in this tin can of a car anyway.

She straightened the wheel just in time. The right back wheel hit the curb. They fishtailed on wet leaves in the gutter before catching the asphalt.

"That was close." Jack heaved a sigh of relief.

"That wouldn't have happened if you hadn't jumped in my car while it was moving and scared me half to death."

"Rather scared to death than shot to death." Jack grinned.

She glared as she blew through streets vacant of traffic that late at night.

Vacant except for a distant wail of sirens.

"About time." Megan flipped on her blinker.

Jack reached across her and flipped it off. "We're not going back there."

"We need to make a statement." In the dashboard light, the perfect oval of her face appeared as white as a bandage, her eyes even bigger and darker than they had been when she dropped from the tree at his feet. "You can't stop me."

"Right. You carry pepper spray." He carried it himself. "But you wouldn't use it against me in a confined car."

"No, but I have a brown belt in karate."

Jack frowned. He'd only made it to yellow. Once he was at the FBI Academy next year, he could advance in his martial arts. For now, he would proceed with working alongside Megan O'Clare rather than against her. He decided to placate her. "Do you want to drive right into what could be a shoot-out with the cops?"

"But—"

"We can give a statement later. Right now, let's just get out of here."

"Us?" She ground her teeth hard enough for Jack to hear across the console, as she slowed for a stop sign this time. "I think you should get out of my car."

"I'd rather not."

"This isn't a rideshare. I don't pick up strangers for rides."

"Jack Luskie, forensic accountant." He pulled a business card from his pocket and held it out to her. "I'm not a stranger now, so let's get going. This isn't a safe place to be at the moment."

She snatched the card from his hand and dropped it into a cup holder on the console. "Not sure my car's a safe place to be."

But Lincoln Park was usually one of the safest neighborhoods in the city due to the high incomes of most residents. Gunshots weren't as common here as they were in his Southside neighborhood, which oddly made him feel more vulnerable.

The four-way stop they were at was clear and had been

since they halted, but she made no move to take her foot off the brake. "I'm not comforted to know your name."

"I can show you my credentials when we're safely away."

"What do you want from me?" Her left hand crept toward the door handle.

She was going to bail out of her own car.

"I just want a ride to the nearest L station." He flashed her his best grin. "Please?"

She shook her head, sending her ponytail swishing across her shoulders. "It's only two blocks away. You'll be—" She gasped.

Headlights flared in the rearview mirror to the accompanying roar of a powerful engine. Behind them, a truck the size of a moving van barreled down the street with no indication the driver intended to brake at the stop sign or the trunk of Megan's car.

"Go. Go. Go," Jack shouted.

No need. Hands back at ten and two on the wheel, she punched the gas and squealed around the corner on two wheels, speeding toward Lincoln Avenue. Good choice. The diagonal street would get them into bright lights and more traffic. More important, they were out of the path of the careless driver.

Except they weren't.

With an agility nothing that big should exhibit on narrow streets, the hauling van swung onto the side street after them. Megan swooped around another corner, the van on her bumper.

"They're chasing us." Her voice was tight.

"Take that alley," Jack said.

Again, unnecessary to tell her. She was already spinning into the narrow gap between a town house complex and a parking lot. The van couldn't follow. The lane was too tight. Lights from Lincoln Avenue glowed ahead. They could get away.

The van roared across the parking lot, smashed down a border of landscaped brush, and blocked the exit from the alley.

Megan slammed on her brakes and sent the little car sailing in reverse, straight as an arrow, twisting the wheel to send them careening back the way they had come, then around another corner in the opposite direction.

"Where are you going?" Jack asked.

"You wanted an L station."

He did. L stations had attendants and gates. A gunman was less likely to follow them into the train station.

Not that shootings at train stations never occurred. They simply did not occur as often as they did in the open streets.

Once was too often for Jack.

"But Fullerton is in the opposite direction," Jack protested.

"And we'll have to cross in front of the van if we go that way."

A few blocks up, but with the lightness of midnight traffic, too easily tracked. Smart lady. Quick thinking.

Fast driving. Someone had taught her defensive driving or at least speed-racing. She swooped around another corner, shot across Lincoln and cruised west. Streets flipped past with lights changing in their favor as though her car were connected to the master switch, or she was good at driving fast and praying hard.

Or maybe not. As they approached Halsted, the nearest train station only two blocks away, the van chugged across the intersection ahead.

She slammed on the brakes. "They guessed we'd come

this way." Megan's exclamation held frustration for the first time that night.

And she said *we*, as though she'd accepted him as a partner in danger. Far better than her thinking he was the bad guy, though she might think that if she knew how he was horning in on her investigation.

An investigation that had gone south in a hurry.

"Turn left and park." Jack pointed left to a narrow side street. "We have a better chance on foot."

"I don't think even Olympic runners can outsprint a bullet." She mumbled the words but swung around the corner and pulled up to the curb in a swift, neat job of parallel parking.

His friends who disparaged women drivers should see Megan behind the wheel.

They piled out of the car and began to move down the sidewalk, not running yet. Running drew too much attention. If he knew her better, he would take her hand as though they were merely a couple heading home from a date. That way, maybe they could prevent their pursuers from finding them, or at least fool them into thinking they were someone else.

"It's too quiet," Megan whispered.

"The bars haven't closed yet, and it's too cold to hang around outside."

"Some of us don't have any choice in the matter."

He grinned at that, but it faded fast as she dropped behind him.

"What are you doing?" he asked.

She didn't answer; she simply took off running, across the street and down an alley.

Olympic running for sure.

Jack took off after her. "Megan, don't."

She tripped on a bag of trash someone hadn't bothered

to lift into the dumpster. Jack reached her and caught her hand before she hit the ground. "Why did you run?"

"How do you know who I am?" She gripped his hand hard enough to hurt.

"I'm working on a case connected to yours. Your name came up."

That was an understatement. Gary had discussed Megan more than Elizabeth Cahill. Bright and fearless. Too fearless for her own good. With Jack having been hired to investigate embezzlement, along with Megan working on Cahill's potential fraud with workman's comp insurance, Gary feared the case might not be as safe as Megan thought. Being the investigator he was, Gary had looked into Jack's background and knew him qualified to keep Megan safe, if he was willing to help, by taking a look in on his subject at the same time Megan looked in on hers. Jack was willing to get a look at Cahill and provide Megan with protection in the unlikely event she needed it.

Unlikely indeed. Jack was thanking God he was there.

He gave her hand a gentle tug. "Let's get out of this neighborhood. That van is only two blocks away."

"And you're right here." She poked a finger of her free hand into his chest. "Why?"

"I'll tell you later. Right now—"

Running footfalls, a pair of them, charged toward the alley. Night joggers, maybe. Doubtful. At best, men up to no good having nothing to do with Jack and Megan. Despite the quality of the neighborhood, crime had begun to spread through its streets. At worst, the shooter from earlier.

Neither of them was inclined to wait around and find out. Still gripping Megan's hand, Jack ran to the patio of a closed restaurant, helped Megan over the low fence, and began to weave through the tables and chairs stacked for the night.

They leaped over the fence on the other side and returned to the street, fleeing down the middle of the asphalt for smoother passage. North Avenue glowed ahead like a beacon. They sprinted for the lights. A train rattled on the L tracks overhead. Something plucked at Jack's coat sleeve a moment after he heard the crack that had nothing to do with the rumble of the elevated train.

A bullet that had come as close as his coat sleeve. A bullet that had missed him by the mere fabric of his shirt. The traffic-heavy street lay a hundred feet away. It felt like a hundred miles. Megan was flagging. Her breathing rasped, and her hold of his hand was growing heavy, like he was a towing line pulling a smaller boat over the water.

And they were being shot at again.

"Let's get off the street." Jack urged her toward the sidewalk. No cars parked here, not beneath the tracks. They wouldn't provide cover. But the darkness might.

Megan's hand dragged on his. She stumbled over the curb, though managing not to fall. Too far to the L despite it being only a block away.

"I wish I could say no one…shoots…on North Avenue." Megan's words emerged in gasps.

"It's more likely they will."

"What?" She stopped, gripping the fencing beneath the tracks. "The noise, of course." She released his hand. "Go on without me. I can't run anymore."

"You didn't throw me out of your car. I'm not leaving you here."

"But they're gone. I can't hear them anymore."

"What can you hear above the traffic?"

She ducked her head. "Nothing."

"Let's go." Jack caught hold of her hand again, and she

moved with him, walking toward the traffic roar, toward the flash of bright headlights and glowing taillights. Too many cars to cross without a light. Waiting for another block and a traffic signal wasn't safe. Waiting on a corner, they were sitting ducks. They could go the opposite way of the L station, but then what?

"Bus." Megan pointed down the street.

High headlights barreled toward them. With a new surge of energy, Megan dashed across the street and began waving her arm at the vehicle. The corner wasn't a bus stop, but maybe the driver would be kind.

He was. With a hiss and squeal of air brakes, the bus jerked to a halt. The door opened, announcing the route number in a sonorous male voice. In a second, Megan leaped up the single step, then spun back, face stricken. "I don't have a fare card."

"I do." Jack pulled his from his pocket and ran it through twice. "Thanks, buddy," he said to the driver.

The man grunted and stepped on the gas. The vehicle lumbered across the intersection just as two people emerged from the darkness beneath the tracks.

Megan grabbed Jack's arm. "The one on the right's a woman."

The man stood with his hands shielding his face. The woman spun away but not fast enough to stop Jack from seeing she looked a great deal like the subject of his embezzlement investigation, like the woman he was certain he had seen murdered not a half hour ago.

TWO

Her heart racing, Megan kept her gaze fixed on the bus windows as though they maintained a freeze-frame of the man hiding his face and the woman who hadn't hidden hers fast enough—a guilty subject, obviously.

But Megan was sure she'd witnessed Cahill's murder. If the woman was alive and guilty, why would she shoot at them? She would want to lie low, pretend she was doing nothing wrong, not draw a ton of attention to herself.

With a hiss and squeal of brakes, the bus paused across the street from the subway station. The door opened. An automatic announcement spoke the stop and bus number. North and Clybourn. Logic told Megan to get off and run into the underground, catch the next train to her neighborhood and the beautiful apartment she shared with one of her coworkers. She could be home in half an hour or less, make a hot cup of tea, wrap in a fleece blanket, and sit on the third-floor balcony to think about the night's events, process them into something that made sense.

But she should go to the police station and file a report. She couldn't remember the exact address but knew it was close, within walking distance of a bus or maybe the next subway stop.

She looked it up on her phone. Or she tried to. Her

fingers wouldn't hit the right keys. Somehow her legs wouldn't settle themselves enough to hold her weight. They bobbed up and down as though performing a sitting jig, and the rest of her body trembled. She grasped a pole for support and started to rise.

The bus door closed. The vehicle hauled into the flow of traffic, and her wobbling legs dragged at her tentative grip, so she tumbled onto the hard, plastic seat.

"Careful." The man who called himself Jack Luskie thrust one arm in front of her as though he feared she would slide onto the floor.

Megan pressed herself against the seat back to avoid contact with that arm, its brawn obvious even in his hoodie sleeve. "I thought you were going to catch a train."

"Not with those goons only a block away." He glanced at her from the corner of eyes as blue as Lake Michigan on a sunny day.

Those eyes were too pretty for his rugged features. Handsome, rugged features. Tall, dark and handsome. Just what she did not want at the best of times, and especially not right now squashed next to her on the bus seat designed for adolescents at best. Certainly not for well-built grown men.

Not that he needed to sit right next to her. The bus was empty besides them. He had a few dozen other choices he could have made. Yet he squeezed onto the seat between two support poles so she had to lean sideways if she didn't want to bump his shoulder with every pothole the bus hopped across.

He looked perfectly relaxed, his long legs crossed at the ankles and stretched into the aisle. Like her, he wore black jeans and black running shoes. Their similarities ended there. His hair was a rich, golden brown like caramel sauce. Thick waves of caramel sauce.

Her stomach growled, and her face felt as red as her hair.

"It's been a while since supper," she mumbled.

"And all that adrenaline works up an appetite once it wears off." He reached into a pocket of his sweatshirt and extracted a handful of miniature candy bars. "Not exactly nutritious, but they're good for a quick sugar fix."

"Thanks." Megan started to reach for a couple of the chocolates, then tucked her hand beneath her. "I shouldn't."

"Take candy from a stranger?" He grinned.

Her stomach felt even more hollow at the sight of curving lips and white teeth just slightly imperfect enough to make them charming and counter the long-lashed prettiness of his eyes.

She stiffened her spine. "I don't know who you are."

From his other pocket, he withdrew another business card. "You left the other one in your car."

This she took and examined beneath the harsh bus lights. The card was plain white card stock with simple black ink printing, the sort one prepared on a printer at home. The name *Jackson S. Luskie* scrolled across the top center in fourteen-point font followed by *Forensic Accountant*. Centered beneath were an address and two phone numbers. No logo or motto, no photo or frills. Blunt and straightforward, like the man himself.

Hmm, this was awful quick to come to a judgment like that. And yet she was certain she was right. Somehow the knowledge comforted her, settled her into thinking clearly.

She drew one of her own cards from her pocket and passed it to him. "Megan Margaret O'Clare."

"I know."

Comfort fled. The two business cards—his and hers—fluttered to the bus floor. "How do you know?"

"My employer told me I might run into you." His gaze was steady, his relaxed pose continuing.

"Then why didn't my employer warn me about you?" she demanded with a little too much ferocity.

He shrugged.

"I can handle a little case of insurance fraud."

"This isn't a little case of insurance fraud, though, is it?"

Megan clenched her fists. "It wasn't supposed to be murder."

"Murder is rarely supposed to happen. But with cases of embezzlement—"

"About which I knew nothing."

"—our work is confidential."

"And mine isn't?" In anger, she found the steadiness to stand, all her warning sensors on high alert.

She didn't want to leave the relative safety of the bus, but she could take a seat in the back near the rear door as an easy escape, should that become necessary.

The bus rocked and squealed to a halt at another stop. A crowd of young men talking loudly pushed their way onto the vehicle and charged to the rear of the bus, leaving the smell of smoke and alcohol in their wake.

She sank onto the seat beside Jackson S. Luskie again.

"Better the stranger you know?" he asked in an undertone.

"Something like that." She rubbed her arms and shuddered. "I think I liked bullets better."

"You wouldn't if one hit you." He touched his right arm.

Megan gasped. "You were hit."

Being so close to him, she hadn't noticed the tear until he pointed it out. Nor could she tell if it was bleeding through the black material.

"You should have said something." She lifted her hand to touch the path of the bullet, thought better of it, and tucked loose strands of hair behind her ear instead. "Is it bleeding?"

"I don't think it even went through my shirt." He drew apart the ragged edges of his hoodie sleeve, and his face paled to a greenish hue beneath the glaring lights. "Or maybe I'm wrong."

"We need to get you to a hospital." She racked her brain to think where the nearest one was. The River North neighborhood? Minutes by car, forever by public transit.

"It's just a scratch. Barely bleeding at all." His grin remained in place, but his voice roughened. "I'll find an all-night pharmacy."

"Where?" She didn't know of any.

"On my way home." He shrugged and winced.

Megan glanced at the card she still held. His home, if near his business, was a long way off, at the far south side of the city. They were sixteen blocks north. He was one hundred and three blocks south. A quick calculation told her he was at least fifteen miles south and probably another two miles west. And he said he didn't have a car.

"I don't think you should wait that long." Megan took a deep breath. "We have to report this to the cops before you go home."

"I'd rather not." He pulled a handkerchief from his jeans pocket and pressed it inside the torn sleeve of his jacket.

Megan fixed her gaze on it, waiting to see if he was bleeding badly enough to seep through the cloth. She would call an ambulance if it did. And then she would call the police about the shooting.

"What upstanding citizen refuses to report a shooting to the police?" Megan asked. "Isn't that obstruction of justice?"

Having the bus driver and even the handful of rowdy youth in the back nearby lent her a bit of boldness.

Jack laughed. "Who said I was an upstanding citizen?"

"You're a forensic accountant. That's a sort of investigator, and everyone in our office is responsible."

"Yes, lily-white northsiders." His tone held a note of bitterness. "You probably don't even have concealed carry licenses."

"I wouldn't tell you if I did."

She did, but the feel of a gun made her queasy, and she never carried one. She had a knife and knew how to throw it with a showman's accuracy, but not a gun. She was proficient enough to pass her PI license and work for Gary, and that was it. So far, she hadn't needed to use any kind of force in her work. Most of the time, she sat behind a computer with online databases spread across the screens of two monitors. But this client required visual proof. Video proof. After days of checking up on the subject, Megan had discovered the time the woman emerged from her house was in the middle of the night. So she'd taken her phone and herself to the nearest vantage point and begun recording.

Recording.

She snatched her phone from her pocket and stared at the screen. She had recorded the woman indeed. She had recorded the couple dining, dancing, then arguing. And Megan had never stopped recording through her tumble from the tree nor the race to her car.

The scent of spicy soap and sun-dried cotton filled her nose a moment before a sense of claustrophobia settled over Megan, and she glanced up to see Jack leaning over her, staring at her phone screen.

"You got better video than I did." Jack thumbed the screen of his own phone to show a handful of blurry images.

"Why do you need pics?" Megan asked. "Why are you in the field anyway and not a stuffy office?"

Jack shrugged. "Curiosity."

"Sure." Megan cast him a dubious glance. "I have to upload this to the cloud and then get a copy to the police."

She tapped the buttons to ensure the video would go to her storage in cyberspace without a Wi-Fi connection. Slow. So slow. And her battery power began to drain as she watched. She had left the house with a full battery, but the video had drawn considerable power. The upload threatened to take the rest.

She stopped it. She didn't dare leave herself with less than twenty percent battery power until she was safely at home.

At the moment, she was headed in the wrong direction.

If Cahill was dead, the insurance company might decide the case didn't need to be solved, and Megan's services would no longer be needed. That commission was all that stood between her and the purchase price of the agency. All she'd wanted since finishing school and going to work for Gary three years ago was her own agency. Six months ago, when Gary decided to retire and sell the company, Megan had asked for first dibs. She had exactly one week to come up with the rest of the money. If she didn't wrap up this case this week, she would either have to ask her parents for a loan or go without making the purchase.

She would rather back out of buying than ask her family for help.

But once the cops took over the case, once Megan reported the assault—murder?—she would be of no use.

Any way she looked at it, tonight's work had lost her the agency.

Unless Cahill wasn't dead. The woman in the street had certainly resembled her. But if it was her, what had Megan witnessed from her tree?

Megan suddenly looked distressed. Not frightened, not annoyed—but almost mournful. As though someone had robbed her of Christmas morning.

"What?" Jack asked.

She glanced toward the window and rose. "I'm getting off."

Jack should, too. This was the last L stop before the bus headed farther west, where the neighborhoods grew less and less safe.

He stood. "Good idea. I can catch a train here to the Loop."

"I'm going to the police. You need to come with me as a witness." Her round chin that lent her face a curving heart shape jutted just a little.

"Do what you like." Jack smiled down at her. "I'm going home before I miss the late bus."

He probably already had, or would by the time he reached the last southern stop on the L.

He would have been better off moving further north. If nothing else, he would save a great deal of time in travel. But office space was expensive in the South Loop, and he had that whole house he had inherited from his parents, with the garden apartment that served well for an office space. And he didn't need to leave his sister alone most days. As of March, the point would be moot anyway. Grace would be well enough to start at her new school in Virginia, and he would be in FBI training.

Grace. He should text her. She should be asleep, but in the event she wasn't, or if she woke and he was still not home, he should let her know he was alive and well.

Not quite well. He did have that wound on his arm. When he raised his hand to pull the stop bell, the gash twinged, and that time he felt himself bleed. Just a little. Enough he probably should get someone to tend to it. Urgent care in the morning. Cheaper that way. Grace's care cost so much that he hated spending a penny on himself, but he did need a tetanus shot.

"You're hurting." Megan's voice was soft.

"It's nothing." Jack shrugged. "Let's go."

The bus squealed to a halt. The disembodied voice announced the stop, and both doors opened. Megan and Jack exited through the front. The crowd of rowdy youth, too young to be wandering the streets in the middle of the night, pushed and shoved their way out the back.

Jack headed for the crosswalk to go into the L station. Megan remained at the bus stop.

"I'm going to call a rideshare." She held up her phone.

The youth who had been on the bus still loitered on the sidewalk where they had gotten off the bus. At Megan's gesture, they stopped talking and eyed her.

Jack stepped into their line of sight. "I'll wait with you."

"You don't have to." Megan thumbed her phone. "I should have a ride in three minutes."

"Just long enough for those kids to jump you and steal your phone."

"I don't want to…" She shook her head, still not looking at him.

"Have anything more to do with me?" May as well get to the point.

She shrugged.

"Whether you say it out loud or not, I know that's what you're thinking."

"Can you blame me?" She glanced up, and in the streetlights, her eyes were big and bright. "You won't go to the cops with me, which makes me think you're up to no good."

"It's not that I don't want to go to the cops with you. I'm happy to give a report tomorrow." He sighed and looked away, embarrassed that he was twenty-eight and worried about missing the last bus like a teen missing a curfew. "I just don't want to miss the last bus home from the 95th Street station."

The car pulled to the curb in front of them, and she opened the door, but kept looking at him. "Where do you live?"

"Beverly. And I have a sixteen-year-old sister I don't like to leave alone all night."

"That makes sense." She appeared to relax a bit.

"Are you coming?" the driver of the rideshare asked.

"Coming." Megan nodded to Jack. "Thanks for helping me escape those people." With athletic grace, she slid into the minuscule back seat.

"But I met you tonight because I need—"

She started to close the door.

Jack saw only one response. He grasped the door and jammed himself into the car. He closed the door.

"I hoped to speak to Miss Cahill tonight," Jack said. "There are so many discrepancies in my files I thought maybe she could shed some light on them."

"But she was never around in the daytime," Megan said.

Jack nodded, then glanced at the driver's back and shut up.

The short trip was made in silence. The driver never said a word, though he glanced in the rearview mirror from time to time, a wary expression in his pale eyes. Jack wanted to reassure him that they weren't the criminals but figured doing so would make the poor man even more uncertain of their legitimacy.

They drove back west and reached the District 18 police station, the nearest precinct. Megan hopped out before the driver or Jack could make a move to open her door for her. She thanked the driver and slammed her door before Jack managed to wedge himself out of the low, tight vehicle. His door had barely shut behind him before the driver sped down Larraby.

Megan was already inside the building and approaching the reception window. Jack lengthened his strides and caught up with her.

"I'd like to report a crime," Megan told the young woman behind the counter.

The station was empty save for an elderly lady asleep on a chair. She was well-dressed and appeared sad even in repose.

Tearing his gaze from the woman, Jack focused his attention on Megan's dialogue with the officer.

"Yes, the shooting off of Armitage," Megan was saying.

"Wait over there." The officer pointed to the chairs and picked up a phone.

Neither Jack nor Megan made a move toward the chairs. Jack knew, and suspected Megan did, as well, that they wouldn't have to wait for long.

They didn't. In just a few minutes, they were ushered behind the barrier and into an interview room. Megan perched on the edge of a chair, arms folded across her front. Jack chose to stand and walk around the room in search of activated cameras or recording devices. He saw both, but neither appeared to be on. He continued to pace. His arm began to throb. Or maybe it had been throbbing and he'd been too preoccupied to notice. He touched it with his left hand. Dry. A good sign. He might get away without mentioning the wound if no one noticed his torn sleeve. And if Megan said nothing.

He caught her gaze and knew she would mention the wound no matter how he tried to ask her not to.

"Why are you so nervous?" Megan asked. "Are you wanted for something?"

"I'll have you know, Miss O'Clare—"

Before Jack could finish his sentence, the door opened to admit a middle-aged sergeant. "So, Jack, are you really reporting the crime, or were you the cause of it?"

"Good morning to you, too, Uncle Dave," Jack said.

"Your uncle is a cop?" Megan leaned back in her chair and laughed. "That's why you didn't want to come here?"

Neither Jack nor his uncle moved.

Megan's grin faded. "So there's a problem here."

"You must be a great PI," Jack muttered with classic Midwest sarcasm.

"Sit down, Jack, and tell me why you're here." His uncle glanced at Jack's arm. "And not in an emergency room."

Jack sat as Megan had earlier—arms crossed over his chest.

She offered Dave Luskie her hand. "Megan O'Clare, private investigator with—"

"I know who you are. That was a nice reception your parents gave for officers wounded in the line of duty."

Uncle Dave being one of them, of course he had been invited to the north suburban home.

Uncle Dave sat across the table. "So tell me what happened this time. Were you the one shooting in Lincoln Park?"

Jack cast him a glare. "No…sir."

"Then may I record this session?" his uncle asked.

Jack and Megan consented, and a red light blinked on in the camera. Since Dave hadn't moved, someone else was listening in.

After stating the date and time and those present, Dave posed his query regarding the shooting in Lincoln Park again.

"We were shot at." Megan glanced at Jack, then took the reins and galloped with the story.

"And now any secrecy for our investigations has flown out the window," Jack said when Megan finished. "Officers will go question Ms. Cahill—"

"If she's still alive," Megan inserted.

"And if we didn't see her killed, she'll be warned her jig is up."

"Sounds too dangerous for civilians to be involved with," Dave said.

"Money says otherwise." Jack looked to Megan. "For me anyhow."

"Not to mention professional integrity," Megan said, but she didn't look convinced.

"You wouldn't need money so badly if you'd let us have custody of Grace," Dave said.

"Over my dead body." Jack spoke through his teeth.

Dave's lips tightened, then he shook his head and moved on from a topic nearly as old as Grace herself. "I want all your case notes and any pictures you have. This is a police matter now."

"My notes are in my car and on the office computer." Megan squirmed. "Can I email my pictures? I really need my phone."

Jack wondered if his uncle could resist the pleading in Megan's moss green eyes.

"That should be all right," Dave said, proving he could not.

Neither could Jack. A glance into those eyes and he thought of summer days on the lake, warm and dreamy, and sharing—

He shook the thoughts from his head. "I can't release my notes without permission from my client." Jack stood. "You'll hear from him tomorrow." He strode to the door, opened it and waited for Megan.

She shook his uncle's hand again, then sauntered past him and into the corridor. Neither of them spoke until Jack and Megan had passed the barricade door and entered the lobby.

"We can take another rideshare to my car," Megan said. "The area might be clear by now. And I can drive you to an emergency room."

"All right." Jack accepted her offer. He was suddenly so tired he could barely stand. His arm hurt. His head hurt. His heart hurt for the loss of his parents and the closeness his family had shared when they were still alive. He hoped Grace would never learn she was the cause of the rift, but he feared she would. Unlike Jack, she believed their uncle and aunt's newfound faith was legitimate.

Megan pointed a finger at his arm. "You should have said something about your arm paining you. We could have gone there first."

"It's just a scratch."

She snorted. "You're not a movie hero." She pulled out her phone. "Let me get that ride called up."

"My turn." Jack drew his phone from his pocket and pulled up the rideshare app he rarely used.

"Jack." Beside him, Megan's voice was tentative. "I suppose I don't know you well enough to ask what that was all about in there?"

"If you knew me well enough, you wouldn't ask." The response snapped from Jack. Immediately repentant, he hastened to add, "I'm sorry. You didn't deserve that."

"I shouldn't have said anything. It's none of my business." Megan glanced at her phone. "Are you upset about losing control of the case?"

"Aren't you?"

"I am. I really need the money." She sighed.

"You're not a trust fund baby?"

"Not until I'm thirty, not that it's any of your business."

"It sure isn't." He couldn't help grinning at her indignation. "I'm just surprised an O'Clare would be so hard up she's concerned about losing her commission on a mere workmen's comp fraud case."

"That's my parents. I don't get a penny from them." She paused in the center of the lobby. "Gary and Janet are selling the agency, and I want to buy it. I need this last commission to have enough in the time frame they require."

Jack opened his mouth to ask why she couldn't just ask her parents, then thought better of it.

"My parents would pay for advancing my education in a minute, but they don't want me to be a PI. It's not highbrow enough for them."

"Let me guess. Law school or med school?"

"Or an MBA, yes. But I'd suffocate in an office, and I like seeing justice done. Were you—" She glanced around the lobby at a handful of newcomers perched on the plastic chairs as though preparing to bolt at a moment's notice, then led the way to the front door. When they stood on the sidewalk again and she'd tapped commands into her phone, she finished her question. "Was that tension in there because your family expected you to be a cop?"

Jack welcomed the sight of another rideshare sign in a car window so he didn't have to pursue that line of conversation. He had already told her more than he'd said to any lady with whom he'd had more than a passing acquaintance. She was easy to talk to.

She was charming. Charming and strong. Two hours ago, they had been running for their lives. Now she was sitting in a crossover vehicle chatting with the driver about jazz versus blues. Nothing seemed to rattle her for long.

A good thing he wasn't going to be working with her. She was too appealing to him, and the last thing he needed in his life was a woman. He would let her drive him to a Red Line L station since that line ran all night, and then say goodbye. The cops would take on the Cahill case now, and he and Megan would no longer be in danger. Then they reached the corner she had given for their destination. Jack saw something was wrong.

Megan's car was no longer parked in what should have been a good location for a few overnight hours.

Even before the rideshare stopped, Megan flung open her door and raced to the empty parking space. "I have a pity sticker. They shouldn't have towed me." Her cry was loud enough to be heard in every apartment on the block. "They shouldn't have towed me."

"They didn't." Jack followed Megan to the opening and saw what she was too distraught to observe.

There, amid a pile of dead leaves in the gutter, lay something white beneath a rock.

Someone had taken her car and left a message with only one word visible beyond the margins of the make-shift paperweight.

SORRY.

THREE

Megan leaped back as though that ragged sheet of paper in the gutter were a deadly weapon.

The single visible word glared at her. "Apology or threat?" she mused out loud.

"Depends on who took your car." Jack crouched beside her. "We can pick it up with a tissue in case they left fingerprints. I have one in my pocket."

"I can do better than that." Megan dug in her jeans and found a plastic bag she had grown used to carrying in the event her roommate forgot a bag when they were out with Tess.

"You have a dog?" Jack asked.

"My roommate does." Megan slipped her hand inside the bag and moved the rock aside.

Jack turned on the flashlight from his cell phone. The words leaped from the page like a slap. No, a blow to Megan's ambitions and maybe even her private investigator license.

LEAVE YOUR PHONE BENEATH THIS ROCK, OR YOU'LL BE SORRY.

"Leave my phone?" Megan shook her head hard enough for her ponytail to hit her on each cheek. "Someone will park here and drive over it and smash it."

"I think that's the idea." Jack slid the flashlight beam around the immediate vicinity. "They want your video or pictures or whatever they think you recorded tonight."

"I know, but they don't know I didn't get the video all the way uploaded to the cloud, and I could have already emailed pictures somewhere." That was what she should have done in the first place. "Smashing my phone is pointless. In fact, I'm going to finish the upload right now, even if it drains my battery to zero percent."

She continued uploading the video to the cloud drive. No one could touch it there.

Unless they managed to take her phone before someone destroyed it, hack into it and delete her files. But they would have to move quickly. Parking in this partially commercial district would be at a premium in another couple of hours.

But the man and his female accomplice could be nearby, watching, knowing if and when she had obeyed their demands.

Megan's skin crawled. Despite the fleece lining of her jacket, she shivered under the sensation of being watched. Every recessed doorway, each tree, every car parked along the street potentially concealed someone surveying her and Jack's moves.

Of course the perpetrators would know where to look. They had taken her car. They knew she would return to retrieve it.

Her car with all her case files locked in the trunk along with her laptop. Password protected or not, getting into the laptop was probably as easy as fetching it from the trunk. Finding an unethical hacker was a mere handful of clicks away on a search. Shortly, if not already, the man and woman would possess information on each of Megan's cases, including the one against Ms. Cahill. She could email a colleague what pertinent data she had on her phone, but without Wi-Fi, that might take too long. And the battery seemed to be draining faster than the upload proceeded.

Arms crossed over her front, Megan scanned her surroundings. Other than a few lights popping on in apartments, nothing in the street had changed. But those lights glowing through shades, curtains and open windows felt like a dozen eyes able to pierce through her skull and read her mind.

"We have to get out of here." Megan barely spoke above a whisper.

Her gaze landed on Jack and discovered he was surveilling their surroundings, as well, one hand in a coat pocket, the other bent behind his back.

Either location could hold a weapon.

So he felt the danger, too.

Without a word, he removed his hand from his pocket and clasped hers. In accord, they started down the street, their footfalls sounding like bass drumbeats against the night stillness. In the distance, traffic noises increased as the morning advanced. Air brakes hissed and squealed. Engines roared. Somewhere a siren began to wail.

Megan wanted to run, locate the nearest open public building and find a corner to hide. Jack maintained a steady pace, not fast, not slow, eating up ground nonetheless. Megan barely managed to keep up. Nausea gripped her stomach, making breathing difficult. Every sense stood on high alert for danger. Her eyes never stopped moving, probing the shadows. Her ears felt stretched from listening for the slightest whisper of pursuit. Her nostrils flared, seeking a change in scent—perfume rather than dried leaves, cordite rather than exhaust. Amber, her roommate, had taught her so much about using her senses for learning her surroundings. Sight was just one. Smell, hearing, taste and touch acquired quantities of information if one employed them.

Megan tasted the bitter metallic flavor of fear. And touch was simply cold, goose bumps rising along her arms, a prickling at the back of her neck.

Then she heard it, the purr of an engine she recognized, a vehicle speeding down the street, too fast for the narrow lane, too fast to be up to anything good. Megan dove between two cars on one side. Jack threw himself in the other direction. No cars for him to take cover on that side, only a border of shrubs as fragile as paper ornaments, not enough to stop bullets.

And the bullets flew. *Bang! Bang! Bang!* Explosions roared from the passenger window.

The passenger window of Megan's own car.

"How dare you," she shouted at the taillights, though not moving from her shelter between two electric cars.

Tears stung her eyes. The red lights blurred, then grew bigger, brighter, closer. The driver had thrown the car into Reverse. Streetlight reflected in a dull gleam from the gun barrel poked through the driver's window.

Megan flattened herself beneath the nearest car a fraction of a second before more gunfire erupted again—from two directions. Too close from one direction. Even closer from another.

Help. Help. Help. Was as much of a prayer as she could squeeze through her head.

Where was Jack?

She edged around beneath the car and spotted him, crouched behind the fender of the next car down, slamming another clip into his weapon.

He really was carrying. And he was shooting. Fast.

Accurate. At least accurately enough for bullets to ring off the metal of her car.

Her poor car was going to look like a colander.

Megan stifled a giggle. Now was not a time to get hysterical. Dark humor would turn to darker tears. She needed to be calm, collected. She took a deep breath. Exhaust and cordite filled the air, as the driver gunned the engine and the car—her car—sped away.

"My car." Half sobbing, Megan crawled from beneath the chassis and scuttled to the sidewalk. Only one thought filled her head: *get out of here.*

But Jack was there beside her, his hand grasping hers to pull her to her feet and help her get moving.

"We gotta get out of here," Jack spoke the admonition out loud. "They can come back."

"That was my car," Megan said.

"Needs a tune-up."

"Not. Funny." After that, Megan saved her breath for running.

They reached the corner and turned. Out of sight of the cross street, Jack stopped and faced Megan. "At the next corner," he said in a murmur, "we'll head for the Brown Line this time."

"But that train doesn't run all night." As she said the words, she heard the squeal of the elevated train running around the curve that carried it north.

"I wasn't thinking about the time." He glanced behind them. "We're safe at the moment, but they could be around any corner by car or on foot."

"Keep running?" Megan clasped Jack's fingers as though she had fallen into a freezing Lake Michigan and they were the only way to climb out before hypothermia took over. Then she followed his lead. More running. More darting between cars and up alleys. They didn't look back. They couldn't hear anyone in pursuit. The tumult of traffic as the city woke up drowned their own footfalls from their hearing, let alone that of others. Every car on the street sent them flattening themselves against the buildings, watching, waiting for danger to strike.

The only scents that filled Megan's nostrils were what rose from overflowing dumpsters waiting for the day's trash pickup. She caught the sound of the truck in the distance, grumbling and whining before the crash of the load spilling into the bed. And always the back of her neck prickled. An attack could spring from anywhere, a doorway, a passing vehicle, around the next corner. They needed more light and more people. They needed time to rest and regroup.

In a lull between traffic and trash collection, they heard it, the click of a cocking gun.

"Where?" Megan asked.

The height of the buildings distorted sound location. She saw nothing out of the ordinary.

Jack didn't respond. Megan understood. Who cared where the gun was? At whom it pointed was what mattered. Finding shelter mattered.

Megan let Jack lead. Her strength was nearly gone. She had been awake for twenty-four hours. She hadn't eaten for ten. Despite her daily runs, her legs ached from keeping up with Jack's longer strides, his greater speed. Every car headlight flared into her eyes like strobes.

This was supposed to be a safe case—workmen's compensation fraud only. Surveillance. Pictures. Lots and lots of computer database searches. She shouldn't be running for her safety, maybe for her life, for the second time in one night.

She could catch her breath at the next corner. They all had traffic lights here.

But Jack didn't stop at the light. Dodging blaring horns and shouting drivers, they cut across the intersection at a diagonal. One car cut so close that heat from its radiator seared Megan's hand.

"I'll take…my chances…with the…gunman," she shouted between pants. "We should just stop and…call the cops."

"Stop where for safety?" Jack's voice drifted back to her, and he clasped her hand tighter as though he could tow her along.

He did. Three more blocks to the L. A few early commuters moved along the pavement with them, giving them odd looks as they raced past. They were a help, though they would never know. Only someone truly homicidal would shoot with others in between.

Jack could slow their pace, but he didn't. He kept up the sprint until the tracks loomed above them and the door to the station rose before them.

Heart banging against her ribs, Megan preceded Jack into the buildings as he held the door for her and three other people. She stopped at the turnstile to see what he was doing.

Three more people entered, then Jack released the door and joined her. "No one's out there," he said. "We might be okay."

Only *might be.*

Megan pulled out her transit pass and scanned it. "Can we walk from here on out?" She glanced down a hallway. "Can we take the elevator up?"

Jack grinned. He wasn't winded, but his hair waved around his forehead in damp curls. So unfair. When she got sweaty, she looked like something one had used for washing dishes. He looked…adorable.

She pushed damp hair off her own brow and headed

for the elevator, along with a few people holding coffee cups. The wonderful aroma nearly knocked her on her back. Her mouth watered, and she suppressed a moan of longing.

But Jack was still with her. "I thought you were going to go south," she said.

"I'm not leaving you alone."

"But they're not around. I mean, we got away from them..."

"As far as we know. They are in your car, so they could meet us at another station."

Megan blinked hard over eyes that felt like someone had applied heavy-grade sandpaper to the corneas. "At least we'll be safe on the train."

Jack wished he possessed Megan's optimism. But she was probably right that the train was likely to prove safe. One never knew whether the nicely dressed man in the opposite seat was a lawyer on his way to work early or a plainclothes policeman riding the rail to ensure the safety of the passengers.

The car Megan and Jack entered held no men or women in business attire that morning. Most passengers, only a handful, appeared to be on their way home from working all night. They slumped in their seats, eyes half-closed, the world blocked out by headphones stuffed inside their ears and phones clutched in their hands. Music cranked so loudly Jack caught the lyrics blasted from the buds of one young man.

"He's either trying to stay awake or trying to go deaf," Jack said, then felt like an old curmudgeon of his grandfather's age rather than a relatively young man of twenty-eight.

Twenty-eight and he was still riding the train for work

because he couldn't afford to spend money on owning a car.

He shook off the moment of self-recrimination and fatigue and checked his phone for messages. Grace would be waking up soon. She wouldn't worry about him, but he texted her to let her know he was all right and would be home soon. Then he texted his elderly neighbor to look in on Grace and make sure she ate breakfast. At sixteen, Grace was capable of taking care of herself except where eating breakfast was concerned. And if she didn't, she tended to grow spacy in her morning classes. Jack figured that meant she should have breakfast every morning, even if her school work was virtual and it was the weekend.

On the face of things, his uncle was right. Grace would be better off living with him and his wife. But neither of their children—now grown men—had turned out well. Far from it. Maybe his aunt and uncle had done everything right as parents, and maybe something in the household was terribly wrong for both sons to end up petty criminals who never held down a job for more than a few months. Jack's uncle had gone to court seeking custody of Grace. She had said no. She was fourteen at the time, and the judge listened to her preference.

But that was before her accident.

Jack returned his attention to his phone. Grace hadn't written back. Not surprising. She liked to sleep.

Beside him, Megan was also texting. Probably her roommate. Her boss. Maybe her wealthy family asking for a new car.

"I think you should tell me what else is going on with the Cahill case." Megan stuffed her phone into her pocket. "Simple workmen's comp insurance fraud isn't worth killing someone over. And your involvement says the fraud is deeper than insurance."

Jack hesitated. He wasn't supposed to say anything, and yet he felt Megan deserved some kind of explanation as to why she had lost her car and nearly lost her life. "A great deal of money disappeared from the company account over the past few months. During the time Cahill has been out sick. Small amounts at a time that add up."

"Embezzlement?"

"Looks like it. She is—" He thought of the crumpled body on the deck, the head lolling oddly, and corrected himself. "She was a software engineer. Hacking into financial records wouldn't be that difficult."

"So maybe the whole slip and fall was a setup so she could be away from the office when the funds began to disappear?"

Jack smiled at Megan, whose face was bright beneath the train's lights. She was a quick study.

"And that's worth—" Megan gulped. "That's worth killing over."

The train slowed to a halt at the next station. He'd forgotten this line had stops so close together on the northbound route. The doors opened. The other passengers in the car exited except for the young man with the blaring music.

Jack eyed the platform outside the open door, watching for others coming aboard, seeking danger.

"One person was just standing there," Megan said after the doors closed, showing him a photo she'd taken of the person. "I don't like that they didn't get on. I mean, it's not like any other train comes this way."

Jack leaned to the side to get a look at her screen. He caught a whiff of her hair. Strawberries and coconut. The fragrance seemed too sweet and innocent for a lady involved in a business that was usually routine and sometimes dangerous. At the moment, the job was dangerous, and Jack experienced an overwhelming need to protect Megan.

Or maybe he simply liked the scent of her hair. And its color. And the way her ponytail bounced around like it possessed a mind of its own. And—

He reined himself in and straightened so he wasn't so close to that shining, sweet-smelling red mop.

"Do you think he—I think it's a he—looks like he's trying to keep people from coming into the car?" Her voice was tight.

She was on edge, alert to danger, not attracted to his unremarkable hair.

"I honestly couldn't tell." Jack glanced toward the door. It was closed now as the train pulled out of the station and proceeded to the next station only a couple of blocks away. "But nothing's wrong with looking at everyone as a potential threat right now."

"Be ready for trouble," he murmured.

She nodded.

With the sun beginning to rise, each golden ray picking out the autumn colors of the trees, trouble seemed unlikely. This was a quiet neighborhood. A safe neighborhood near a locally venerated university. No one would try to harm them in breaking daylight.

The train slowed. Stopped. The doors glided open. Jack was on his feet and backing toward the end of the car before a passenger with his hood up stepped off the platform.

"Don't move," one of them said.

But Megan was already moving with Jack behind her, shielding her from the newcomers to the car. She flipped up the latch to open the emergency door. The roar of wheels on tracks swirled around them with the rushing wind dozens of feet above the ground. The walkway in between cars was short but narrow, with the infamous third rail providing thousands of volts of electricity to power the trains running along one side and the service platform on the other. The space didn't allow for errors like a slip or a stumble.

Ahead of him, Megan stepped across the gap and shoved through the door into the next car. Jack started to follow. A hand shoved between his shoulder blades.

And Jack stumbled out of the car and began to fall toward the third rail.

FOUR

Jack wasn't behind her. He had been so close to her for hours she sensed the absence of his proximity even before the train door slammed behind her.

"Jack." She spun on the heel of her trainer and grabbed for the emergency release.

He was there, beyond the window, between the two cars. And he wasn't alone. Another man was trying to shove him over the guardrail toward the deadly third rail.

Jack was a big man and seemed strong, but his arm had been injured, weakened. The other man was also big. Not as tall, but even broader than Jack. He appeared as though he spent hours at the gym on the weight machines.

The man from the deck. The man who had possibly killed Cahill with his bare hands.

"Help him," Megan cried—to whom, she didn't know.

No one on the train appeared to be anyone who could help. A handful of tired-looking women, a sleeping teen, a man in a suit. They all stared. None moved.

Megan shoved through the door and grabbed hold of the burly man's belt. She thought she was strong when working out on a weight machine. Faced with true strength pulling against her, she may as well have been a house cat trying to take down an elephant.

If only she did carry a gun…

She would never be able to shoot anyone. And yet one could bash someone over the head with the barrel.

If she carried a handbag, she could club him with that. But handbags got in the way when climbing trees or running…

The man she tried to stop had carried a gun earlier. He concentrated on Jack, seeming to not notice her feeble efforts to stop him. He couldn't hear her over the rumble of wheels on track, echoing off buildings above the rush hour roar of traffic below, sirens wailing in the distance, wind whipping past at gale-force speed.

Megan found the man's gun holstered beneath his coat and yanked it free.

"Hey." He jerked around, towering over her, swaying with the rhythm of the rails. His face was red with effort or rage or both.

Megan gripped the barrel of the pistol and swung the stock toward his face. A second before steel met bone, he grasped her wrist.

"I don't think so." His voice rose above the tumult.

"You…don't…think." His words coming between gasps, Jack snatched the gun from Megan's fingers and tossed it onto the platform. In seconds they left it behind, a piece of evidence of the night's work.

And the man was gone, too, slamming through the emergency door and vanishing into the car.

"You're all right." Megan started to sigh with relief.

Then a hand clamped onto her shoulder and spun her around. "What are you doing, young lady?"

"You." Megan came face to coat buttons with the suited man from the train car. In the hand not holding her, he held a badge.

A train cop. She knew they existed to keep the public

transit system safer but had never met one. Now she was closer to one than she liked—one who obviously didn't pay much attention to what was going on around him if he hadn't heard her cry for help.

He scowled at her beneath an upper lip needing a shave and eyes so tired they appeared hollow, haunted. "I asked you a question, miss."

"Someone was trying to push my friend over the railing." She turned to point toward Jack.

He wasn't there, either.

He had invaded her case, scared her out of a tree, which had got her shot at, hitched a ride in her car without her permission and jumped into her rideshare without asking. And now, when she risked her life to save him, he'd vanished on her the moment a cop appeared.

She was beginning to see a pattern. Jack Luskie didn't like the police. She didn't understand that of a man with light brown hair and blue eyes, unless he was lying to her and was a criminal, not a forensic accountant.

"Maybe he went after the man who pushed him." She spoke to herself as much as to the cop.

"Then let's go find him." The officer steered Megan to the only door through which Jack could have disappeared.

But he hadn't disappeared. He sat—slumped—on one of the forward-facing seats near the exit doors a third of the way up the car. He held his arm, and the bit of his face she could see appeared a little on the green side.

He hadn't abandoned her; he had gone to sit down before he fell and accomplished the other man's task without him having to do anything. So Jack was probably not a criminal?

Relief so profound her knees weakened flowed through Megan. She sped up the aisle, tripping on a suitcase someone had left in the way, and sank onto the seat beside him. "Do you need an ambulance?"

"I'll be all right in a few minutes." He released his arm.

Blood smeared his fingers.

Megan shuddered. She didn't really mind the sight of blood. She simply didn't like it coming out of people she felt responsible for.

Which was ridiculous. She was in no way responsible for a grown man who was at least half again her size. And yet…

"You two are off at the next station," the cop said.

No problem. They had missed their transfer point and needed to backtrack anyway.

He stood in front of them, arms crossed over his broad chest and above an equally broad belly. "We can't have people on the trains who are fooling around between cars."

"We weren't playing around," Megan protested. "We're not stupid."

The cop's raised eyebrows said he thought differently.

"Someone was chasing us and tried to—"

"Forget about it, Meg," Jack interrupted. "He can't help us."

"But the—" This time, Megan interrupted herself.

This officer of the law, probably near retirement and figuring the train patrol was an easy gig, wouldn't be able to do anything about the gun on the platform, the possible murderer somewhere on the train, the danger she and Jack were in on and off the L. They would call Jack's uncle when they got somewhere safe.

If they got somewhere safe.

Megan wasn't sure where safe was. Her office? Her apartment? Jack's house? These people could know very well who she and Jack were and where they worked and lived.

Where they lived.

Megan shot upright. "I have to get home. Now." The slowing of the train came as a relief. "My roommate's all alone. If someone shows up there, she might get trapped. Hurt."

"Call her," Jack said.

Megan held up her phone. One per cent battery power.

"Use mine." Jack handed her his phone.

Megan raised her eyebrows at the phone's age but said nothing as she tapped in her roommate Amber's number. Ringing began…and repeated…and repeated.

Nothing to worry about. Amber couldn't always get to her phone. She might not want to answer the strange number so early in the morning. Nothing was going down in Megan's third-floor walkup. Nothing.

The train brakes squealed to a stop. Megan sprang to her feet, tossing Jack's phone into his hand. "I've got to catch that train going in the other direction." Dodging commuters made twice as thick by backpacks or wide by oversize messenger bags, skirting a newspaper machine and a stairwell, she reached the other side of the platform in time to leap onto the train a hair's breadth before the doors slammed shut. The night had come to an end. She was hopeful she could go home and rest and leave the Cahill incident to the cops.

Jack gnawed on the inside of his lower lip as Megan sprinted from his life and Grace gabbled on the phone.

"Don't worry," she said, "I'm sure it'll be all right, but…"

The *but* was the problem. The worry.

A strange car had been idling in front of their house

for the past hour. The rumble of its engine had awakened Grace, who slept in the living room downstairs because she couldn't manage steps.

She had been unable to see the car's license plate. She didn't know one car make from another. It was dark. Compact. The windows were tinted enough so she couldn't see any possible occupants in the early-morning light.

"I'm sure it's all right," she reassured him. "I just thought you'd want to know."

"I do."

But not when he was more than half the length of the city away. He could do nothing to save her.

She wouldn't be alone if she lived with us, he heard his uncle saying.

And she'd probably be running wild in the streets.

Except now she wasn't running anywhere, not through any fault of her own. Not through any fault of his, Jack knew in his head. In his heart, he felt guilty for letting her go on her first date with a boy he barely knew. She was sixteen, after all. He'd dated at sixteen. And they weren't alone. They were with an entire group of young people attending one of the city's numerous festivals. Jack could no longer remember which one, just that it had been somewhere public transit didn't easily reach, so someone's parents had offered to drive them in their van, a rarity of a vehicle in the city.

Not one person in that van was responsible for the other festival goer, who had been drinking all day before driving himself home. He'd T-boned them as they left the street on which they had parked. T-boned them right where Grace was sitting.

Other kids were injured, along with the parents. Grace's legs had been badly broken, and she suffered a head injury that had put her in a medically induced coma for nearly a month.

Her legs would heal. She would walk again, but probably not run. The doctors were sure she would even lose her speech impediment with therapy. Her spirit, on the other hand, was still an iffy matter.

Her friends had come around often during the summer. Now that school had started up again, their doorbell rarely rang, and Grace was no longer buried in her phone texting or on some social media app. She read far too much for a teenage girl who had once only done her homework because she knew she needed to, not because she liked it.

Schoolwork seemed to be all that engaged Grace now, that and learning how to knit. An occupational therapist said it would be good for restoring her fine motor skills. And so it had been. Grace was good, to Jack's untrained eye. At least he could help her with math.

And he could keep her safe.

"Grace," he asked in as neutral a tone as he could, "have you noticed anyone near the house?"

"Just some guy reading the meter."

Jack shivered on the warm train. A meter reader could be legitimate. It could also be someone checking out his house.

How had he found it anyway? Oh, yes, Megan's car. She had tossed aside his business card. The thief—the killer—could have gone to his house to intimidate him—or Grace, once they figured out she was there.

"Grace," Jack said with a little more urgency, "stay away from the windows. In fact, close the drapes."

"But that makes the house so dark."

"I don't care. Just do as I say."

"Is something wrong?" Her voice shook.

"Maybe."

Of course something was wrong. He had good reason to believe she was not safe at his house, yet she was safer staying there than trying to go anywhere on her own.

"Just listen to me," he said. "Please."

"All right." Sighing, she agreed.

He left the train station and flagged a cruising taxi. It would cost more than a rideshare, but it was there, not on the other end of an app he would have to navigate and then wait to accommodate him. The driver's face lit with happiness the moment Jack gave him the address. The fare was going to cost a mint.

He texted Grace his estimated arrival time and asked if the car was still there. She responded that it was and she was staying away from the windows.

If I could get upstairs...

She didn't finish the thought. Jack understood. If she could climb stairs, she could probably read the license plate from an upstairs window.

Give it time, he wrote back.

A cliché everyone told the frustrated sixteen-year-old all summer. *The bones will heal with time. The pain will go away with time. Your tongue won't feel thick if you give it time.*

He and the therapists and doctors were right, but Grace wanted to be well now. She wanted to go to school and have friends again.

The problem was, in March, Jack was uprooting them anyway when he entered the FBI Academy. She would go to a boarding school in Northern Virginia, where she could be close enough for him to visit, yet be well taken care of and have classmates with whom she could make new friends, away from those who had hurt her.

He'd been saving for the school fees for a year. Every penny from their parents' life insurance had gone to pay Grace's medical expenses. He had intended it for her college tuition. Now he counted on selling the Beverly house for her future. He didn't need the money for himself. His future was securely planned.

An image of Megan flashed across his memory. When the time came for him to marry and have a family, once his law enforcement career was settled and Grace's future was assured, Jack hoped he'd meet another woman like Megan wherever he was assigned. He liked her spirit.

He would have ensured she reached her door without incident if Grace hadn't called. Megan seemed secure enough when she entered the train. If her walk home was short, she should be fine in broad daylight. Should be. But what about Grace and the idling strange car, and the suspicious meter reader?

Lips pressed in a thin line, he stared out the window at the masses of cars crowding the side streets the cabbie had taken. An old-timer, apparently, he knew the backways to avoid the worst of rush hour, though nothing helped in the narrow, old streets overflowing with too many vehicles for their width. Even the L trains they passed under looked packed to the gills. So many people smashed together made Jack restless. Any one of them could be dangerous, and not necessarily the ones people thought were dangerous. The man at Cahill's had looked wealthy, maybe a little uptight, with his tucked in polo shirt and tailored slacks above loafers and no socks. His hair had been cut short, but Jack couldn't recall its color. Brown? Dark blond?

He shifted on the cracked vinyl seat as he tried to force

his mind to recall every detail. He couldn't. But Megan had pictures and a video on her phone. Jack didn't need to remember.

He should have called his uncle to have someone go to the house and check out the vehicle idling in front. That way, he could have walked Megan home and assured her safety. She was in danger until she got that video uploaded to the cloud or to another electronic device.

But that would have meant admitting to his uncle he wasn't one hundred percent capable of ensuring Grace's safety. If Grace wasn't safe, Jack wasn't a good guardian or brother. If he wasn't a good guardian, he should let his uncle and aunt have custody.

He leaned forward, peering through the windshield as though doing so would make the taxi move faster. They were making good time considering the hour and the distance. Fifteen miles could mean as much as an hour.

But, no, they were turning onto 103rd Street. Not much farther…

At last, they reached his street and turned. Jack peered down the block to his house. Several cars and a couple of trucks lined either side of the road. One truck was running as its driver checked a utility line. So was one of the cars.

"Stop here." Jack was already swiping his credit card through the machine, as the cabbie stomped on the brakes.

"You're okay here?" the cabbie asked. "The GPS says it's another block."

"It's fine." Jack gave the man a generous tip for getting him there so quickly, stuffed his card into his wallet, and slid out the door.

He didn't tell the man he doubted he was all right there. Worse, neither was Grace, not with Megan O'Clare's car idling in front of his house.

FIVE

The four blocks between the L station and her apartment proved an exercise in extreme observation for Megan. She didn't merely look into the face of everyone she passed—a considerable number because of the time of day—she found herself stopping every quarter block to look from the tops of the buildings around her, to the pavement she had already traversed, to the gaps in between houses, for signs of danger. What that danger looked like she didn't know. She simply felt it in the hard oblong in her pocket—her cell phone. Until she uploaded that video to another computer, to a server where others could access the data even if her phone was destroyed, she doubted she would feel safe.

While crossing the third alley along the route, she peered along the passage, counting dumpsters and other hiding places for someone with a gun, and she wanted Jack with her. He had been an imposing presence, with his height and his apparent strength. Not to mention his lighthearted way of speaking to ease tension.

Tension was no good in her work. Tense people made mistakes. She couldn't afford a mistake.

She started to pull her phone from her pocket to text him, then realized she had lost both his business cards.

That was silly of her…and disappointing. His business should be listed somewhere. She looked it up under his name online but only found an office number with electronic voicemail, not his cell phone.

She would have to wait to see if he got in touch with her. Not that he had any reason to now. Or ever.

Another disappointment. Nothing she should worry about. She needed to worry about her case now being in the hands of the police. She could make her report to the insurance company, but if Cahill was dead, they had no one to pursue for recompense for moneys paid out through fraud.

If she was dead, Megan needed to figure out who had been their female pursuer.

Head spinning, Megan reached her building. She fed her key into the lock and entered the minuscule foyer. The smell of her neighbor's curry lingered in the confined space, and Megan's stomach growled. She hadn't eaten in hours. Too many hours. She was so hungry she doubted she could manage the forty-two steps up to her flat.

She started to pause and gather the mail she saw through the window in her mailbox, then grew aware for the first time that the front door was mostly glass. Not even plate glass. Just window glass. A bullet would smash through it in a second, and the shooter could be gone before anyone other than Megan realized what happened.

The thought spurred her up the first fourteen steps to the landing and the source of the delicious smells lingering from one more tasty dinner the night before. Another fourteen steps took her past a neighbor she never saw. Mail disappeared from the mailbox, so he or she or they had to come and go, but no one knew if one or six people lived in the flat even after the year Megan had been there. She took the final fourteen steps to her apartment door, unusually winded because of fatigue and hunger. Normally she considered the several trips up and down each day her workout. She no longer huffed and puffed when she reached the top flat.

Megan, Amber, and Amber's dog, Tess, shared the entire top floor. A broad balcony in front and a sunroom in the back kept the place from seeming claustrophobic. Not to mention a dozen large windows.

The scent of coffee greeted Megan before she slipped her key into the lock. The instant she swung the door open, doggy toenails scrabbled on the wood floor and Tess streaked around the corner from the kitchen to the hallway and flung herself at Megan's feet, rolling on her back, four paws in the air, tail swishing.

"You silly thing." Megan bent to rub the dog's belly to the accompaniment of snorts of puppy glee, though Tess was four and a half.

Golden retrievers were forever puppies.

For two seconds, Megan considered dropping onto the floor beside the dog, wrapping her arms around her, and letting Tess lick away her tears.

Then Amber appeared around the doorway from the kitchen. "Meg, I hope that's you."

"It's me." Grammar disregarded, she changed her focus from dog to roommate and colleague.

Amber was small, with hair the color of her namesake, and gray-blue eyes that moved as though she were restless. In truth, it was a medical condition she couldn't control and which prevented her from focusing. That was how Tess had come into her life—as her guide dog. Megan had yet to find a part of the city Amber and Tess couldn't reach on their own.

At the office, Amber was a combination of receptionist and research assistant. She had moved to Chicago from

Pittsburgh for the job and needed a place to live. Megan had needed a roommate. They had been inseparable ever since.

"Is everything all right?" Amber asked. "I mean, you were out all night."

"Everything is anything but all right." Megan blinked at the mist in front of her eyes. "I got shot at, my car was stolen, and—"

She had met a gorgeous man.

"You're kidding." Amber caught hold of Megan's shoulders. "At least I hope you are."

"Not a bit." Megan rested her head on her friend's shoulder. "And I had to rescue a man from getting pushed off an L."

"I think you have a lot to tell me." The understatement was so Amber that Megan started to laugh, albeit a little hysterically.

"Can you feed me something besides a banana smoothie and coffee? I won't have the strength to talk if I don't get real food."

"If you make it good with the boss if I'm late."

"Since I'm practically your boss…" Megan began, but maybe she wouldn't be after all. "Let me plug my phone in and text Gary we'll both be late. I need to tell him about my car and laptop." She sighed. "The rest will wait until we get into the office."

"Not for me it won't, if you want breakfast." Amber headed back to the kitchen, Tess on her heels.

"I will. I will." Megan stumbled down the hallway to her room.

Because her room in the house she had grown up in had been frilly and full of priceless antique furniture, Megan's current room was modern shabby chic. She'd purchased every piece from a secondhand shop or through ads posted on a neighborhood app. The result was cozy comfort, not showpiece angst. An overstuffed chair in moss green microfiber graced one corner. Megan dropped her messenger bag beside it and plugged in her cell phone on the round table between that and her bed. She considered dropping onto the chair for a moment's rest, decided she might fall asleep there, and headed for the shower instead.

She wanted to linger beneath the hot spray but hurried through ablutions and dressed in black leggings and a black-and-rose print tunic. Her hair went into a messy bun. Only because her reflection told her she looked sickly pale, she brushed on some makeup before exiting to the café table in the kitchen.

"Can I do something to help?" she asked, already knowing the answer.

Amber scooped eggs from a pan onto a plate. "Stay out of my way."

"I can butter the—"

"I have the toast."

Amber was intimidatingly efficient in the kitchen. She complained that nothing she made looked like the videos online, but who cared about presentation when the flavor was so magnificent? Megan hadn't learned to cook growing up, so she was self-taught and not well. Somehow, her efforts neither looked like nor tasted like she thought they should.

As Amber glided toward her, Megan rose to take the plate of scrambled eggs and toast. Coffee and juice followed, and she didn't say a word until she had scraped her plate clean and started on the second cup of coffee. Then she told Amber her story as concisely as possible.

At the end of the recital, Amber said, "Tell me more about this Jack guy."

"I nearly get killed, and you ask about a man." Megan pushed her plate aside and thumped her head on the table. "I don't have time for men in my life unless they are clients."

"That's why your voice goes soft whenever you say his name." Amber stood. "Why don't you get some sleep. I'll clean up here and get to work."

At the word *work*, Tess wriggled out from beneath the table and ran to the door. She loved her job.

Megan smiled at the dog, then all but crawled to her room. Part of her mind told her to go into the office. The rest warned her she would be worse than useless if she didn't get some sleep.

She was asleep seconds after she pulled the duvet over herself.

Jack called 911 and reported sighting a stolen car. He hung up before the operator could ask him how he knew the car was stolen. He needed to get off the block before the utility truck moved and exposed him to the driver of Megan's car.

He had grown up in the neighborhood, had run wild most of those years, and knew every highway and byway, every nook and cranny. He knew which gangways between houses he could traverse and not get stuck in a backyard, who had a dog to look out for, and which routes kept him hidden from the street.

Selecting a circuitous route, he ended up at his back gate. Normally, he could climb the fence. This morning wasn't normal. His arm throbbed, and the rest of him didn't feel much better.

So he called Grace to let him in. She grumbled about having to put on shoes but was grinning when she managed the two steps from the back stoop to the ground with her walker.

Oh, she looked good. Strong and so pretty he knew he would worry as much as any father when she went back among people and found herself another boyfriend or gaggle of admirers. He wanted it to be soon for her sake and forever for his.

"Is the car something bad?" she asked him.

"Yes. I'm glad you warned me." He entered through the gate she unlocked and hugged her close. "The cops will come and take care of them soon."

He hoped.

"Who are they?" Grace turned on the walkway and headed back to the house, trying not to drag her right leg.

"It's a stolen car." Jack didn't want to tell her more.

"How do you know?" She asked the question, as he knew she would.

"Long story I'm too tired to tell." He strode ahead of her so he could open the back door. "One reason why I was out all night. I was making a police report. Among other things. Saw our uncle."

"And he wants me to move in with them." Grace thumped her walker into a corner of the kitchen and made her way to a chair with the help of the counter, then the table. "Says I'd be better off there."

"Something like that." Jack eyed the coffee maker. They needed to get out of there, but he needed to do it in a way that didn't alarm Grace. "Sure you don't want to go? You wouldn't have to leave Chicago and everyone you know."

Grace stared at the table, her long, wavy brown hair shielding her face. "Why would I want to stay here? It's not like anyone is friends with me anymore."

"They will be once you're in school. Want to go out for breakfast?"

"But you can't distract me with an invitation to your favorite diner. I know my friends are afraid I'll want to go places with them, and I'd embarrass them."

"Oh, Grace." Jack didn't know what to say. From what he'd seen, he feared she was right.

But she was the same person—smart and pretty and possessing a good sense of humor. She was strong in mind and body and held a determination he hadn't known she harbored.

"So I'd rather start over again," Grace continued. "And I'll be close for you to visit when you get days off." She flashed him her brilliant smile. "Besides, I can brag my big brother is a fed."

"A boring accountant."

"Not if you're chasing stolen cars." She glanced toward the living room.

Jack slipped through the curtains he'd hung between the dining and living rooms for Grace's privacy so he could look out the front window.

The car was there, no longer running, and empty.

Jack began a systematic check of all the windows and doors, seeking signs of tampering, of telltale wires. He should get himself and Grace out of there. The car wasn't parked out front for no reason, even if it was just some kind of warning or twisted joke. Maybe he would check things outside, but first he must take time for a quick shower and change of clothes.

So maybe Grace would be better off with his uncle. The man seemed to have changed since he and their aunt had resumed going to church after twenty years or so away.

Jack's job wasn't supposed to be dangerous. No one

went after forensic accountants. Most people never knew who they were.

If only he hadn't allowed Farrel to convince him Megan needed looking after, he wouldn't be in danger, too. He and Grace. Megan would have done fine on her own. Maybe better if he hadn't startled her from that tree. But then again, he was glad he had been there so she hadn't faced such a scene alone....

Then you wouldn't have ever met Megan.

He turned the volume off on that little voice in his head. He would do quite well not knowing Megan. He simply needed to call her to tell her about the car showing up in front of his house. He only knew her office number and doubted she was there, but he would call her office to have whoever was in get a message to her.

But first he needed to look around the outside of his house to see if anything was changed.

Ten minutes later, he had his answer. With the flashlight on his phone giving him a view beneath the meter, he spotted the scratches. They weren't from normal wear and tear; they were fresh, sharp to the brush of his fingertip.

Someone had tampered with the meter. Or tried to. Jack didn't know which and didn't want to wait around to find out. He had to get himself and Grace out of there.

She was capable of traveling on public transit. Buses had ramps and train stations had elevators. Better than staying in the house where she wasn't safe. "Do you want to go with me today?" he asked Grace.

The way her face lit was answer enough.

"Just one question," Grace asked as they exited the house through the back door, avoiding the abandoned car out front.

"One of many," Jack muttered.

"For now," Grace conceded.

"What is it?" Jack scanned the area for signs they were being followed.

"Why are you taking me with you?"

Jack shrugged.

Grace glared.

Jack sighed. "All right. All right." He scanned around them as he and Grace headed for 103rd Street to catch the bus. "The man you saw at the meter may have tampered with it."

"You mean they were trying to hurt us?" Grace's voice squeaked.

"Something like that." No sense in lying to her.

They reached the corner. Others waited for the bus, as well. Jack said nothing more. He watched the group. He watched the street, ready to snatch Grace up at a moment's notice. Their journey began without incident. Bus. L train. Crowds of people. Jack insisted a high school age boy move so Grace could have a seat. His thought that kids were born without manners these days made him feel old—too old to be picking up and relocating to another state to a new life that would have him moving often, more likely than not. Unfair to Grace?

But she'd be in high school, then college, then a life of her own. This was his calling, what he was meant to do. He had been so sure since he applied for a place in the academy. Grace's accident had been the only glitch. He'd had to delay his plans. But not cancel them.

He leaned against the train car wall in front of Grace, watching passengers, watching platforms.

Seeing nobody suspicious, Jack looked up Megan's office on his phone. Less than a block from an L station. Good location. A long ride for them, but no trains to transfer to. No more buses. Not much of a walk. And somewhere to go with Grace, someplace public and safe.

He could tell Megan in person that someone had tampered with his meter. Explosives weren't his forte, and he didn't know what danger a wired meter posed. Nothing good for sure. Something to stay away from. A warning at the least.

Grace had settled back with a book, though she occasionally glanced out the window at the city flashing by until they dove underground. The noise increased, rumbling train wheels echoing off the tunnel walls. More people crowded on again and again, shoving handbags and backpacks into Jack until he thought he would suffocate. Then they reached the Loop and the crowds began to disperse. The car emptied with each stop back out of downtown until only Jack and Grace and one other man were present. Jack seated himself beside his sister, never taking his gaze from the other passenger. He appeared to be sleeping. Jack knew better than to trust that pose. Sleeping dogs didn't always lie asleep even if you didn't mean to wake them.

The train swept from underground.

"One stop to go after this one," Jack told Grace.

She nodded and slipped her book into her backpack. It was purple, but Jack had carried it for her so much in the past few months he didn't care if people gave him odd looks.

He shouldered it now and offered her a hand up. She shook her head and steadied herself with her walker as the train slowed. The doors slid open, and a blast of smoke-scented air and the hint of a haze blew in.

"This is terrible. What's going on?" Grace said.

Jack didn't know, and his gut warned him he didn't want to know. But he had to find out.

"Grace, wait right here on the platform by the elevator. Don't move."

Further back in the station and protected by the superstructure of the elevator, the air was clearer.

"But—"

"Please."

"Okay, but leave my bag."

He hooked the strap on her walker, then took the steps down two, three at a time, the address of Megan's office on repeat in his head. *Thirty-two something North Sheffield. Thirty-two something North Sheffield. Thirty-two...*

What was the something?

Jack feared the answer wouldn't matter.

He would find out the truth in a moment.

The crowd on the sidewalk stopped him from moving. Beyond them, fire trucks and police cars stopped the crowd from surging forward. Taller than most present, Jack rose on his toes to see over the crowd as far as he could.

And spotted smoke pouring from the building he was positive contained Megan's office.

SIX

Smoke and the stench of burning gas filled Megan's office just as she and Gary finished looking over her video from the night before. Down the hall, Tess began to bark and Amber screamed.

Fire. Someone had started a fire.

Megan sprinted for the lobby. Amber was a capable woman, and Tess a stellar guide, but these dogs weren't trained to get people out of burning buildings, were they? Good sense should have Tess guiding Amber away from the worst of any flames and smoke. But which way was that from Amber's reception desk? The fire could have cut them off from the front door or from the hallway and back exit.

Megan slammed to a halt at the reception entry. She saw no flames, but the smoke was black, billowing too thick for her to know where to find a clear path to safety.

She began to cough. "Amber," she called between gasps for air.

She tugged her T-shirt over her face. The cotton was poor protection but better than nothing.

"Amber," she tried to shout. It was more a croak.

"Megan, come out this way," Gary yelled to her, his own shirt tied around his face.

"Amber," Megan repeated the name.

"You can't go in, and we've got to get out of here."

"But we can't leave them in there. They aren't answering." From smoke or distress she didn't know. Maybe both.

"We'll do better getting them through the front door." Gary tugged on her arm. "I have the backup drive."

"I'll go get Amber."

"You're not big enough to be helpful. Take this." Gary thrust the flat box of the backup drive toward her. "You get out."

She took the hard drive from Gary and raced for the door into the alley.

Gary was twice Megan's age, and not as fit. If necessary, he wasn't capable of carrying Amber and Tess. Neither was Megan.

The wail of a siren told Megan they might not have to do any rescuing. Help was on the way. A fire engine, a police car, an ambulance.

Not the ambulance. Please, God, not an ambulance.

The silence from the lobby shook Megan's belief the two could be all right.

Because of me.

Okay, because of her case. Because of the wrong the man and woman had committed that went beyond workmen's compensation fraud. Still, she had pushed it because she wanted the agency.

The agency that was, at that moment, burning. Burning in the middle of a block of other businesses all connected. Others could suffer. Others could lose.

Head down, she burst into the sunshine and shadow of the alley. A trash truck idled at the nearest end of the alley, unable to exit due to the emergency response vehicles lining up along the street, and the throngs of people crowding the sidewalk. Megan ran in the other direction. A glance back told her Gary hadn't followed.

Because he'd gone directly to Amber. She knew it without him telling her. No other explanation for his absence. He wouldn't have gone to his office for papers. He hated paper files and kept everything digital he possibly could. Digital and duplicated.

But Tess and Amber were his responsibility as far as he was concerned. All the women he hired were.

Except he had let Megan go out on her own while feeling the need to rescue Amber.

Megan nearly smiled. Amber wouldn't like that. Appreciate it, yes, but not like it.

Gasping for air from the run more than smoke, at the end of the block, Megan drew her shirt from her face, glad she had worn a tank top beneath. She paused long enough to gulp fresh air, then sped up the block and around the corner…

To nearly mow down Amber and Tess.

"You're safe." Megan hugged her roommate.

Tess nudged her way between them.

"How did you get out?" Megan asked.

Amber gave her a "well, duh" look. "When the window shattered and smoke filled the room, I grabbed Tess's harness and told her, *Outside*. She took me right to the door. I couldn't even see my hand in front of my face, but maybe the smoke was thinner at Tess's level. But I think she'd still know where the door is." She patted the golden on her head.

Tess's tail waved like a plumy flag behind her.

"We'd better go tell Gary you're all right. He was going back into the building for you."

"He should have known—" Amber smiled. "He's such

a good man." She gestured with her hand, and she and Tess faced the way they had come.

"Why don't you wait here." Megan glanced toward the office. A solid line of people, mostly first responders, blocked the sidewalk. Smoke reigned over their heads like a canopy of gray gauze. "It's crowded up there, and I'm afraid Tess will get trampled."

Amber nodded. "I'll wait here."

"Back soon." Megan trotted up the sidewalk toward the office, toward the source of the smoke. Smoke and probably fire from a homemade bomb someone had shot through the window. To intimidate her? To destroy the office? Surely the perpetrators knew the video Megan had taken would be secured by now.

But if she were dead, she couldn't verify anything from the video, and it was dark, unclear.

She hefted the backup hard drive beneath her arm. She should have taken time to drop it into the safe. That was fireproof. Even so, the physical drive was only insurance against something going wrong with the remote backup or if internet service went down for a while and they needed old data. Whoever had chased her the night before, stolen her car, tried to push Jack off the train, might not even be behind the fire. They'd left others disgruntled with their work. In most investigations, someone came out the loser.

But in the thirty years Gary had been in the business, no one had ever perpetrated a physical attack, so she doubted this one was related to anything else.

Megan paused beside a utility pole to survey the organized chaos ahead of her. She couldn't find Gary. From shouts from the first responders, she knew they were allowing no one near the building. Gary hadn't emerged. Megan should try to get someone's attention to assure them their receptionist/researcher and her dog were safe, but their boss was not.

She shoved the hard drive down the front of her shirt to free her hands, then gripped the pole and stepped onto its base for added height in her search for Gary. "Gary," she shouted.

No one could possibly hear her above the tumult of commands, running engines and onlookers.

"Gary." She waved her arm.

Someone caught hold of her wrist and began to tug.

"No." Megan gripped the pole with one arm wrapped around its rough surface and kicked out with her right foot. If only she wore boots. Running shoes weren't much good as defense weapons, especially when her foot failed to make contact. The pressure on her arm increased. She tried to look at her attacker. He wore a sweatshirt, hood up, hiding much of his face. Bushy eyebrows bristled forward from beneath the black hood, thick and dark like those on the man from the video.

"Help." She cried the word. Uselessly. Her voice sounded too quiet, too strained with her effort to maintain hold of the pole and pull herself free.

Her arm felt stretched, the socket yanked to the breaking point. She tried to scream, but no saliva wet her mouth enough for sound.

"Why?" she rasped.

The man seemed not to hear her.

Amber was only a block away, but she couldn't see that far to know what was happening. Everyone else focused on the fire. Megan kicked out again, connected with someone solid. He grunted, then gave her another yank. Megan lost her grip with her right hand. Her left arm flopped limply at her side. She forced it to move, to lift, to protect the backup drive inside her shirt.

"Let me go." Instead, he tossed her over his shoulder. Then he began to run toward Amber and Tess.

For a brief moment, Jack had spotted Megan struggling to hold onto a utility pole while someone grasped her arm and attempted to haul her away. But then the crowd shifted, and his view was obscured.

Jack began to push through the crowd. Her name hovered on his lips, but not even the loudest shout could be heard over the throng and the wail of sirens. Hemmed in on all sides, he was tempted to begin lifting smaller people out of his way. No point. He doubted that would get him there faster. First responders were arriving. They were equipped to help.

But Jack was closer. He needed to be there. Every sense in his body told him he needed to get to Megan.

He sought a way around the crowd.

Jack glanced behind himself for another route. Of course. He should have thought of it sooner. It would take time, but not as much as trying to fight forward, risking getting waylaid by the police—or worse.

He spun on his heel and began to charge back to the L. Access card in hand, he scanned it as he leaped over the turnstile. An attendant shouted at him. He ignored her. He'd paid even though he wasn't riding on the train. He took the steps two, then three at a time.

And raced past his sister.

"Jack," she called to him, "where—"

"Just wait. I think you're safe here."

He hoped she was. She was so far. The station was filling up. No one would hurt Grace in such a crowd.

He paused to see if Grace was indeed all right, if anyone was taking notice of her. She seemed fine. Secure.

From the advantage of his elevation and height, he swept his gaze over the masses of people below…

And saw Megan struggling as a man carried her away over his shoulder.

He took the opposite steps in a few leaps, nearly fell over a baby carriage blocking the bottom, as if the mother intended to haul it up two flights of stairs rather than take the elevator, and jumped over it without doing anyone harm.

"Sorry," he shouted to the shocked mother.

Then he was out of the station and all the way around the block from Megan. But the block was nearly empty. Empty enough for him to maintain his headlong dash.

He couldn't keep up that speed for long, not without any sleep the night before, not without much food for at least eighteen hours. No matter, he had been a champion runner in high school, the one thing that had saved him from being a hoodlum, and he'd kept up the running since.

He reached the end of the block and swerved around the corner. A block away, a woman and her golden retriever stood against a building. The dog sat gazing up at her, ears pricked up at full mast, as the woman rested one hand on the dog's head and moved the other along her handbag as though she were playing a piano on the leather. To Jack, racing toward her, she appeared anxious, worried.

Call 911, he wanted to shout to her.

He saved his breath for this block. Megan was nearby unless the man had dragged her into one of the buildings. Possible. Unlikely. Anything could have happened in the five minutes she'd been out of his sight. Five minutes that felt like five hours.

He reached the corner and jogged across the street without looking for traffic. An air horn blasting sent him jumping onto the opposite curb. Twenty feet away, the dog rose, positioning its body between Jack and the waiting woman. Jack waved, hoping the woman would understand he was no threat, and looked up the block.

The man ran toward Jack, mere yards away, with Megan tossed over his shoulder as though she were being saved from a burning building.

The man kept coming, head down as though he intended to plow right through Jack. Jack planted his feet and waited. One yard closer. Two.

He heard Megan's voice now, hoarse and maybe angry. "You can't do this. You need to let me go."

No panic, just admonitions.

In spite of everything, Jack grinned. Then he waited until the man was a yard closer and kicked high and hard. He wore only running shoes, but a solid kick was a solid kick, especially with the man's momentum throwing him into the blow. It caught him in the solar plexus. He stumbled back. Megan threw her weight to the side.

The man staggered, then dropped her. She sprawled on the pavement like a discarded sack of grain.

The man regained his balance and swerved around Jack, breathing hard enough to be heard above the background cacophony.

Jack cast Megan a glance, longing to help her up, ensure she wasn't seriously injured. A thrill at seeing her again overrode the longing. Then he took off after the would-be kidnapper.

The man stumbled and glanced Jack's way. For an instant, he caught sight of thick brows and a heavy jaw inside the hood, then the man took off again. Jack kept after him, nearly got his hands on him.

But an SUV pulled to the curb at the next corner. The man hopped in the open passenger door, and the vehicle sped off, tires squealing around the corner, cars honking, brakes slamming cars to a halt.

Jack bent double, hands on his knees, breathing hard. He needed to write down what numbers on the SUV he remembered. With those and the make and model and color, the cops could possibly track it down and catch the man, along with the woman at the wheel. Jack couldn't describe anything about her other than the long, blond hair, like Cahill's.

"But we saw her die," Jack muttered to himself.

Or maybe they had not.

Jack turned toward Sheffield and the ladies he had left behind there, trying to maintain a brisk pace when he wanted to trudge like a kid on the way to school. That last run had sapped his energy. His head spun with fatigue and hunger.

And he had to retrieve his sister, left behind on the platform like a dropped newspaper.

He dug his phone from his pocket and called her.

"Where are you?" she greeted him.

"A block away. I'll come get you—"

"I'll get myself." Her tone was clipped, a little irritated. "I'm on the street level now."

"I told you to stay."

"And I'm a bad dog."

"Don't disrespect your elders."

She snorted, then said something a passing train overhead drowned in its rumbling roar.

Jack reached Megan and the lady with the dog and nodded at them, pointing at the phone. "Will you please stay at the station so I can escort you…somewhere?" he said to his sister.

He had no idea where to go now.

"I have to go to the office," Megan said to him or maybe her friend. "I need to check on Gary."

"Who is that?" Grace asked.

"Megan."

"Megan, is it?" A tension had crept into Grace's voice. "Maybe I should go home."

"You can't."

Jack understood why she wanted to. Society wasn't always kind to those who weren't apparently "normal" in body and/or mind.

He glanced at Megan again, talking to her friend, and wondered how she would treat Grace. Part of his mind had registered the harness on the golden retriever, telling him the woman was visually impaired, and Megan talked to her as he had seen her talk to others—as though her friend's disability meant nothing to her.

He found himself hoping she would treat Grace that way. Then he mentally kicked himself for caring how she treated Grace. Well, of course he cared. Despite the strength of her faith, Grace's fragile self-confidence didn't need someone snubbing her when she stumbled over words or forced one to move slowly. Yet a tiny prick of light, of warmth, inside Jack warned him he wanted Megan to give Grace the right reaction for his sake, as well.

He admired her. That was all. He didn't want to be disappointed, though he admonished himself to remember that everyone carried clay feet somewhere in their character.

"Wait in the station, please," Jack said. "I'm not sure it's safe."

"If you insist." Grace's voice was small amid the background noise of hundreds of people, blaring loudspeaker announcements, and train doors ringing the warning they were about to close.

Jack disconnected and looked at Megan. "We still have a perp to catch," he said.

"Before he kills us," Megan conceded.

SEVEN

Megan felt sick. Guilty. If she hadn't insisted on finishing up the Cahill case any way she could, hadn't gone out in the middle of the night and climbed a tree to spy on her case subject, Jack never would have been attacked on the train. Her car wouldn't have been stolen. The agency wouldn't have been bombed. No matter that she had been attacked, nearly kidnapped in the midst of everything else.

She covered her face with her hands, tried to breathe deeply, slowly. She concentrated on not being sick there in front of Jack, which would be too humiliating to endure, or give in to the dizziness taking over her head. She felt as though a puff of wind would knock her onto the pavement in a heap of slacks, shirt and running shoes.

"Megan?" Amber's voice sounded far away.

A large, warm hand slipped beneath her elbow. "Let's find a place you can sit down," Jack said.

"There's a nice coffee shop down the street," Amber said.

Amber. Jack. She hadn't introduced them.

She lowered her hands. "I'm all right. Thanks. Amber, this is Jack."

"The accountant." Amber smiled and held out her hand.

Jack took it. "That makes me sound boring."

"I don't think you and Megan have had a boring time of it in the past few hours," Amber said.

"Twelve hours." Megan looked at her phone. "Only twelve."

She noticed a man in uniform walking toward them. The fire captain, she suspected.

Megan held up a hand. "I need to talk to this guy."

"And I need to get my sister."

Megan paused in midstride forward. "Your sister?"

"I thought she was safer with me than alone, considering your stolen car ended up outside my house and someone tampered with my gas meter."

Though she knew her foot landed on the sidewalk, Megan felt as though she had just stepped into Jell-O. "My car?"

"Why don't we go back to our apartment," Amber suggested. "We can have lunch, and all be quiet and safe away from chaos."

"I think a cabin in the woods sounds like the right call at the moment." Megan rubbed her temples.

Surely her ponytail was too tight, affecting her brain and what she was hearing. Her car couldn't possibly be in front of Jack's house.

"How did they know where you live?" Megan asked.

Jack shrugged. "Probably my business card left in the car. How did they know which car was yours parked on the street?"

"They saw it when they chased us out of the neighborhood."

He touched her arm, a mere graze of fingertips, encouraging, reassuring, not at all intrusive. "That fire captain looks impatient. Let's head that way. I'll go meet Grace at the station and wait for you there."

"Sounds good." Megan glanced behind her to ensure Amber and Tess followed.

They did, Tess's nails clicking on the concrete, her head up, her tail again waving behind her. She looked proud of herself. Amber looked concerned, tense around her eyes and lips.

More guilt slithered through Megan. She was making everyone unhappy. And if this all hit the news, her parents and siblings would find out. Talk about unhappy!

She met the fireman and a cop halfway up the block. Jack waved and kept going. Megan crossed her arms over her waist.

The fireman nodded at her when she approached. "Someone pointed you out as an occupant of the building."

"What do you need to know?" Megan asked. "What happened? Have you seen my boss, Gary?"

"Your boss went to the hospital for smoke inhalation, but he should be fine," the fireman said.

"You're sure?" Megan was shaking. "I mean, he's not young. And the stress… The office? Is his office destroyed?"

"It was a homemade incendiary device. Fortunately, the carpet in the office has a fire retardant in it and you have more smoke than fire damage. We didn't find many flames or serious damage, but the structural integrity will have to be inspected before you can use the office again."

Megan shook her head, which was spinning at the number of tasks she now needed to take care of with Gary temporarily out of commission.

This is what you want, she reminded herself. *Being*

boss means more than giving directions to others and collecting a commission on every case.

If she ever could become the boss in a permanent way.

"Do you know why anyone would do this to you?" Another man joined them. He wore a suit with no tie and an open top button on his shirt. "Detective Ryan," he added.

"Megan O'Clare." She sighed, picturing a visit to the nearest precinct, hours in an interview room drinking bad coffee and again explaining what had happened the previous night. Unless she could simply refer them to Lincoln Park.

"And, to answer your question, yes, I do believe I know," she answered at last. "I think it has to do with one of my cases."

The police officer and the detective looked interested, but the fireman gave her some instructions as to what her next steps should be, then returned to his crew finishing up inside the office.

"I'll need a statement from you," the policeman said. "Names, if you have them. When. Why."

And that someone had tried to kidnap her from the fire scene?

Yes, she should probably report that to him, but in a split-second decision, Megan decided to wait until she reported at the station. Telling them now would probably get her hauled to the station at once for no good reason. The man was long gone.

"May I give you all the details later?" Megan stared at her grimy clothes, at the bulge where the backup drive still rode inside her shirt above her waistband. She needed to sit down and think things through. "I need to get our receptionist and her dog home first."

Behind her, Amber snorted.

Megan cringed. She hadn't quite told the truth there.

She didn't need to get Amber home, not strictly speaking. Amber was capable of getting herself home, thanks to Tess. But Megan wanted to escort her home, wanted to keep her friend safe.

"And I have people waiting for me," she added, which was one hundred percent the truth.

"You can come into the station later." The detective spoke with deliberate slowness. "But I need to know how to reach you and anyone else who's a witness."

Megan gave him her business card, scrawling her cell number on the bottom, and pulled out her phone to bring up Amber's. "She was the closest to the bomb."

The cop's gaze swept from Amber, to Tess, then back to Megan. "That's all right."

"I'll come with Megan to make a statement later today," Amber said, an edge to her tone.

The cop didn't acknowledge her.

Megan gritted her teeth before saying, "And you can contact Sergeant Dave Luskie at the Eighteenth Precinct about what went down last night. That will save us all a lot of time."

With that, she nodded, then turned to Amber. "There's a mess up ahead. Do you want an arm?"

Amber hesitated, then reached out her right hand for Megan's elbow. With Amber holding Tess's leash for a heel on her left side, Megan guided them through the rest of the detritus on the sidewalk, then the few onlookers who remained. On Belmont, the crowds were thicker and moving faster, hurrying to and from numerous restaurants for lunch. Red and Brown Line trains rumbled overhead, adding to the cacophony, so neither of them spoke. A pall of smoke mingled with the aromas of grilling burgers and frying doughnuts, making Megan at once nauseated and hungry. Most of all, she was tired, and the bone-deep, soul-deep fatigue made her feel like she carried a fifty-pound pack on her back. Every survival instinct told her to go home, crawl into bed and sleep for about twelve hours.

But not business survival. She had a hospital to contact about Gary's condition, other agents to call and tell the office was temporarily closed. A cleanup crew to contact and schedule. Worst of all, she needed to have the building inspected for serious damage. Of course, they would need to replace the carpet and possibly furniture in the lobby. The sprinkler system had likely gone off and damaged computers and other office equipment. That meant calls to the insurance company.

She tripped on the curb in front of the L station.

"I think I need to be guiding you," Amber said with a chuckle.

"Tess's better at looking where she's going than I am." Megan scanned the crowd. "Where is Jack? He's so tall, I should be able to—ah, there he is."

He stood next to a bench outside the station. Since he said he was meeting his sister, Megan wasn't surprised to see the young woman beside him. An older teen with utterly stunning looks. A more delicate, feminine version of her brother, with his clear blue eyes and curly, golden brown hair worn in a high ponytail. And in front of her stood a walker.

He hadn't mentioned his sister had walking difficulties.

The closer Megan drew to the pair, the more she noticed lines of pain around the young woman's lips.

Though the trip must have been an ordeal for Jack's sister, he had brought her to keep her safe.

Because of one case that should not have been important in the scheme of things.

Megan doubted she could smile without it coming off as forced, so she merely held out her hand to Jack's sister. "Hi, I'm Megan."

"Grace." She took Megan's hand in a soft, firm grip, then smiled, her whole face lighting. "I'm sorry my brother has caused so much trouble."

"Me?" Jack exclaimed. "That's hardly fair."

"He's…a troublemaker all the time," Grace pressed on, her smile metamorphosing into a grin.

Megan noted the hesitation in Grace's speech—slight, but noticeable to someone trained to observe details. She loved how Grace teased her brother. Megan's elder brother had teased her when they were young, before the race to enter the best schools, Ivy League preferably, drove them apart because Megan wasn't interested in that route.

She no longer had difficulty smiling at Grace. "Give him a break this time. I think the trouble came from me, unless his scaring me out of that tree started all this."

"I was trying to help you," Jack protested.

Megan rolled her eyes, then introduced Amber.

"I think we should go back to our apartment," Amber said. "We can have lunch and…" She trailed off, her right hand touching Grace's walker. "But we're four blocks from the L. Is that too far to walk?"

"Yes," Jack said.

"No," Grace said at the same time.

They frowned at one another.

Jack shrugged. "It's up to you, but we still have to get home afterward."

"Or to the police station," Megan pointed out. "Amber and I have to make a statement, and you should probably come, too."

"I should." Jack scrubbed his hands over his face, looking even more fatigued than Megan felt. "I saw that man dragging you off, so they'd probably want to talk to me."

"What man?" Grace asked.

"Long story." Megan yawned. "Or maybe not so long. Just distressing."

"Is it going to bring Uncle Dave back into things?" Grace asked.

"Probably." Jack held his hand out to Grace. "If you think you're up to this, let's get going."

"We could take a rideshare," Amber suggested.

"Too much trouble with this thing." Grace patted her walker with her hand. "And I need the exercise."

"We can take our time." Megan turned toward the station door. "We live near the Bryn Mawr—oh no. That station doesn't have an elevator."

"And neither does our building," Amber said. "How thoughtless of us."

Grace ducked her head, cheeks growing pink. "Sorry to be so much trouble."

"Sorry the rest of us are so far behind the times." Megan touched the girl's shoulder. "We're just fine staying around here."

They ended up at a café down the street from the station, with coffee, water, sandwiches, and awkward conversation all around the table. In bits and pieces, Megan and Jack explained about the man who had nearly kidnapped her, tossing details they'd seen or experienced back and forth like a ping-pong ball, as though they told stories together all the time.

All the time, when they had known each other for little more than twelve hours. The longest twelve or thirteen hours of Jack's life—other than those after Grace's accident, when he had been unsure whether she would live, then whether she would walk or remember her own name, let alone his.

And now she was doing so well, talking with ease to Megan and Amber.

Because they had made her comfortable. Neither had reacted oddly to her walker or her slight speech impairment. They noticed. They wanted to accommodate for Grace's needs and left the issue at that. Natural. Accepting.

Jack had little time in his life for friendships with women, let alone dating, but the few times he had dated in the past year, the women had been so uncomfortable around Grace, he had never asked them out again. Grace was his sister, his ward. He needed anyone with whom he spent time to treat her like a thinking, intelligent person.

As Megan had.

Not that he would date Megan.

He gazed at her across the table. Despite the dark circles beneath her green eyes, she was still so pretty. She wore no makeup he could detect, yet her skin was creamy and flawless, her lips a natural pink and so quick to smile.

Under other circumstances, he might want to get to know her better. But he was leaving the state in less than six months, embarking on a new life that provided no room to care about anyone beyond Grace and himself for years to come.

And surely only his weariness was making him think such absurd thoughts about getting to know Megan O'Clare. She might be the rebel in her family, but he doubted she was that rebellious. Ladies from North Point did not date men from Beverly even in the twenty-first century.

So they would get through this crisis created by the events of the previous night, and then say goodbye.

That settled in his mind, he realized someone had asked him a question. He straightened his posture and grabbed his glass of water for the chill of the ice-filled vessel. "I'm sorry?"

"I asked you if you agree these people need to be rid of us because of what we saw," Megan said, one eyebrow raised.

"Definitely. They couldn't get your phone in time to stop you from sharing the video, so they want to get rid of an eyewitness."

"Weren't you an eyewitness, too?" Grace asked.

Jack sighed and nodded in reluctant admission.

"Then won't they want to hurt you, too?" Grace's speech halted more than usual.

"That's why I brought you with me today." Jack saw no need to lie to Grace. Forewarned was forearmed. Except she couldn't defend herself if anyone tried to harm her.

"This is messed up," Amber muttered.

"We'd better get to the station and make our reports." Jack reached for his wallet to pay his half of the bill.

"It's taken care of," Megan told him, her cheeks a little pink.

Jack narrowed his eyes at her. "When did you do that, Miss O'Clare?"

"When you were dozing." She smiled and rose. "I'm going to order an SUV to get us to the train station. Take your time coming outside."

She left, Amber and Tess following.

"What was that all about?" Grace asked.

Jack gave her a questioning glance.

"Don't play stupid, Jack. You called her Miss O'Clare like she's twice your age, not the nicest lady you've met in a thousand years."

"She paid the bill, like I can't."

"So she hurt your pride by being nice. Maybe she just has more money than she thinks we do."

"She comes from money."

Yet she'd said she needed this case so she could afford to buy the agency. A woman with access to her family's funds wouldn't need to do that.

So maybe she was just being nice.

"I wasn't sleeping," was all he could think to say.

Grace laughed. "Practically snoring into your plate."

He pretend-punched her arm, then stood so he could help her up. The table didn't look steady enough for her to use it as a brace while she pushed herself to her feet. By the time they reached the sidewalk, an SUV idled at the curb, Amber and Tess in the far seat, and Megan in the third row.

"I hope this is all right," Megan said. "He said he has a portable step if the running board is too high still."

Such nonchalant thoughtfulness of Grace.

Jack forgot his annoyance with Megan. "I'll just lift her in."

Grace settled, Jack slid between the captain's seats to sit beside Megan, though the third row had surely been designed for children, not men over six feet tall.

And Megan was too close—close enough for him to catch a whiff of fresh shampoo from her springy ponytail. Something that reminded him of Christmas baking. Gingerbread men. That was it. Warm, ginger cookies his mother used to bake.

"All settled?" the driver asked.

With everyone's assent, he closed the door and walked around to the driver's side. In moments, they pulled into traffic and headed down Belmont. Reluctantly, Jack took out his phone and texted his uncle. He hoped the older man was still asleep, having worked all night.

He wasn't. An answer popped back immediately. He would come to the station at once. And pick up Grace.

Of course he would pick up Grace. The problem was, Jack couldn't argue with him this time. She was safer with their aunt and uncle than with him. Someone had already tried to kill him twice. The stolen car left in front of his house and the tampered meter were the last straw. Another attempt on his life might catch Grace in the crossfire.

Only until this is over, Jack responded.

He didn't realize he murmured the words until Grace twisted inside her seat belt to look at him. "Only what?"

"Uncle Dave is coming to pick you up. You'll stay with them until we get this all straightened out."

"And what do we do in the meantime?" Megan asked.

"Leave town?" Amber suggested.

"I can't," Megan said. "I have to run the agency, and you wouldn't believe all the things I have to do to get the office up and running again."

"And I have a business to run," Jack added. "I'm self-employed. I can't afford to just drop everything."

Jack looked at Megan. Their eyes met, held. Hers blazed like green bulbs on a Christmas tree. Jack's burned, not from fatigue, but from the intensity of his feelings regarding the situation into which they had been thrust, and something else niggling with a thread of intensity. Before he could examine that, before he could say anything, they reached the station and didn't have a chance to talk at all.

A young officer, following orders, insisted Grace and Amber remain in the lobby.

"But I'm a witness," Amber protested.

"Sure, ma'am." The officer addressed Jack. "The two of you can come back."

"Ma'am," Amber grumbled behind them. "I'm only twenty-six."

"She is a witness," Megan was saying.

"But she couldn't have seen anything," the officer said.

"She can see some, and she could hear and…" Megan trailed off and sighed. "Let's worry about Amber being left out later and get through this."

They got through it in separate interview rooms, as though they might tell different versions of the incidents that day if they weren't together. Of course, their stories weren't the same. They each had a different perspective. By the time they finished talking to separate sets of officers and reconvened in the lobby, Jack wanted to go for a long, hard run or go to a gym and hit a punching bag.

"They dismissed my concerns like I'm some hysterical Victorian maiden." Megan spoke Jack's thoughts aloud, her eyes flashing.

"Same here," Jack said.

Grace giggled. "They treated you like a hysterical Victorian maiden?"

"Practically."

"In short," Amber said, "they didn't take you seriously."

"They think the attack on the office was mere vandalism from a disgruntled client or spouse of a client or something," Megan said, toe tapping a jig rhythm on the tile floor. "And I was nearly kidnapped by someone who saw an opportunity to steal my handbag and the hard drive."

"Because that happens all the time in Lakeview," Jack grumbled.

He dropped onto the hard chair beside Grace. "My uncle told them the video you sent doesn't show enough to be useful, even serious."

"And my car getting stolen?" Megan asked. "How do they explain that?"

"Cars get stolen all the time in this city." Jack patted the chair beside him. "Have a seat. We can talk a little while my uncle brings his car around front."

"What's there to talk about?" Megan lowered herself beside him as though her muscles ached from head to toe. "How it's coincidental my car ended up in front of your house?"

"We can try to figure that out," Jack said. "But I was thinking we should talk about how we are going to figure out what's going on and who is trying to do us in, if no one else is going to take us seriously."

EIGHT

Megan gave her head a violent shake. "Neither of us is qualified for that kind of an investigation."

"I don't think either of us is eager to die, either." Jack's response was immediate, as though he had already planned for her objection. "I have a future ahead of me, a sister to get back into high school and training to do at the FBI Academy."

"And you want to run the agency," Amber added.

"You two are ganging up on me." Megan shoved her fingers into her hair, loosening her ponytail so it drooped to one side.

She felt like drooping to one side, keeling over and hiding under one of the stained and shredded chairs in the stark police station lobby. Surely no criminal would come to find her in a cop shop.

And her calling wasn't to hide. If she truly wanted to hide from the world, she would have sheltered herself inside the overblown halls of some corporate law firm helping big, soulless companies grow even bigger.

"I can't think right now. I need to—" She trailed off as the sergeant from the night before strode into the lobby and straight to them.

Jack rose. "Afternoon, sir."

Respectful but cold. Jack didn't like this man for more reasons than his desire to take over guardianship of Grace.

The two men shook hands, appearing as though they were having a gripping contest rather than a friendly greeting.

Grace didn't move, said nothing.

Megan arched her brows and nudged Amber. "What's up here?" she whispered.

Amber shrugged. "Someone just turned off the heat, that's for sure."

"Turned it up, more likely." Grace struggled to her feet. "Hi, Uncle Dave. Nice of you two to offer me a place to stay for a few days."

"Your aunt is home getting everything set up just right for you. You'll have a real bedroom and your own TV—"

"I need some things from home, like my computer," Grace interrupted.

Megan guessed why she had been so rude. Jack's lips had compressed into a hard, thin line, tight enough for a white line to show around them, and the tips of his ears burned. Anger? Embarrassment?

"You can't go home. I don't think it's safe." His tone was as tight as his face.

Anger. Embarrassment, or perhaps simple anxiety for his sister's safety.

"Someone tampered with our meter," Jack continued.

Another volley of exclamations and recriminations erupted. Luskie sent someone scurrying with orders to do something. Grace accused Jack of treating her like a child who couldn't know the truth. Jack said nothing until the room fell silent.

Megan also decided to run interference. "Thank you

for coming, sir." She rose and held out her hand. "Will I get my car back?"

"Eventually." Sergeant Luskie shook Megan's hand with the right amount of firmness. "Forensics will go over it first, but I doubt we'll find anything. We haven't found anything anywhere else." He shot a glare at Jack. "Nothing on that video that identifies anyone clearly enough for facial recognition software to match him with anyone. We can't get a warrant to check the Cahill residence without some kind of probable cause."

"So you think this is all nothing, too?" Jack demanded.

His uncle shrugged. "Someone did steal Miss O'Clare's car. We can't rule that out."

"And parked it in front of our house," Grace added. "I saw it myself. It sat there running forever."

"With no one in it," the sergeant said.

"Why?" Megan asked. "Surely they were thinking something besides a mere warning."

"Checking the place out." Jack looked pale. "Or they didn't make a move because Grace was there. Or they hoped whatever they did to the meter would finish the job, and they wanted you to know who was behind the attack."

"Some criminals will stop at hurting children." Luskie picked up the purple backpack. "This yours, Grace? We need to get going."

"Yes, sir." Grace sighed.

She smiled warmly at Megan and Amber, patted Tess on the head with an embarrassed "Couldn't resist those big brown eyes," by way of apology, then held her arms out to her brother. "Take care of yourself."

"I will." Jack hugged her back, leaning down so she could whisper something in his ear.

He nodded, returned some remarks to her, then straightened. "Keep her safe, sir." He watched them all the way to the door and as far as they showed through the plate glass window. Not until the tall man and small young woman disappeared from view did he turn his attention to Megan and Amber. "Can we go to your house to talk? This isn't the place."

"And we have good coffee." Amber wrinkled her nose. "Whatever they're serving here can't be healthy."

"If any coffee is healthy," Megan said. "Not that I should talk, when I drink the stuff like other people drink water."

"Same here." Jack strode forward and held the door open for Megan and Amber.

They made their way to the nearest L station, noting how cold the weather had grown. Cold and cloudy, as though maybe they would get snow in October. Not unheard of.

Megan rubbed her arms inside her lightweight jacket. She would have to get out a winter coat if the temperature dropped further. Where she stood, several floors above the street and within a mile from the lake, the wind held an edge.

Beside her, Tess raised her muzzle and sniffed the east breeze.

"What is it?" Amber asked. "Smell rain or snow?"

"Careful using that word." Jack zipped the front of his hoodie. "I'm not ready for winter."

"This is the Midwest," Megan said. "I'm ready for winter from the middle of September. I mean, look at Tess. She's had her winter coat since the end of August."

"Virginia will be warmer," Amber put in. "Congratulations on getting accepted into the academy, by the way."

"Thanks. I was supposed to go a year ago." The train arrived. In the middle of the afternoon, seats were plentiful. Amber and Megan shared a forward facing one, and

Jack sat behind them, continuing his story. "Then Grace had her accident, so I postponed it."

"Will she stay with your uncle while you're gone?" Megan asked.

"No." The single word was delivered in an explosive, decided burst.

Megan wasn't about to ask him what the problem was. He could tell her in his own time or not. It was none of her business. She didn't even want it to be her business. She had enough family issues of her own to manage.

Especially when someone in her family saw the pictures of her office bursting with firemen in the newspaper or maybe even on the news. Probably just the paper. They weren't important enough for the TV news unless some enterprising reporter figured out who she was—an O'Clare of North Point.

Megan asked about Grace's accident, since Jack had brought it up. He explained about the van rolling over, overcrowded so Grace wore no seat belt. She'd been trapped beneath the van seats, her body twisted and broken.

"Her recovery is astounding," he concluded. "And she improves all the time."

"But steps are out of the question?" Megan asked.

"She can manage one or two, but not a whole flight. My house is two stories with only a living room, dining room, and kitchen on the first floor, so I made her bedroom in the living room."

The reason why their uncle had made that dig about Grace having a real room to herself.

Megan shook her head. She was used to competition between brothers and sisters, but not between uncles and nephews.

She wanted to say something to prompt a confidence

from Jack, but drops spattering against the window of the L train distracted her.

"So much for no rain in the forecast," she grumbled. "Does anyone have an umbrella?"

None of them did. They descended from the L platform on steps growing wet with the increasingly thickening rain. Tess paused to shake, then put her head down and began trotting toward home. The rest of them followed suit, minus the shake. Heads down, they charged along the sidewalk, shoes and jackets soaking through. By the time they reached her building, Megan's hands were so cold she could barely get the key in the lock. She dropped it twice. Jack retrieved it both times and stuck it in the lock the second time. The door swung open to a puff of warm air smelling of old wood and fresh paint.

"Be ready to climb," Megan said, heading up the steps. "I make this trip several times a day. It lets me eat ice cream when I want to."

And Jack's sister never could have gotten as far as the second floor.

She loved her apartment but found herself wondering if she should move into a building with an elevator so Grace could visit her.

Which was a ridiculous idea. She would probably never see Grace again.

At that moment, reaching her apartment door, she wondered if maybe she should move into a building with an elevator anyway and run more miles on the days she took the time for a jog or went to the gym. Every muscle in her body trembled as though she had used up that day's reserve of energy and was borrowing from the next day's to keep going.

Behind her, Amber and Jack didn't appear much different. Only Tess seemed undaunted by the day's excitement—

exertions. She shook with vigor, spraying all of them, even though they were already soaked.

"Towel," Amber said.

She allowed Tess to guide her through the door Megan opened for them and headed straight for the laundry room and the stack of faded and frayed towels they left on a shelf especially for the purpose of drying off the dog.

"I think I need one, too." Jack stood on the welcome mat, water dripping from his jacket and hair and the tip of his nose. Megan experienced the oddest impulse to brush those drops off his face.

She suppressed it and headed to the linen closet. "You get a human towel."

She exchanged the towel for his drenched jacket. His shirt was damp beneath, but the jacket seemed well-waterproofed.

"You can leave your shoes by the door and come into the living room. We have a gas fireplace."

"Nice place," Jack said.

"I fell in love with it the first time I ever saw it." Megan busied herself dusting off the top of the fireplace and flipping the switch. With a whoosh, the flame ignited around the artificial logs. "I could never afford it without a roommate. And it's cheaper than it looks because we are half a mile from the L and you have to walk up a gazillion steps to get here."

"Nice view." Jack stood at the French doors leading to the balcony.

"It's a beautiful city." Megan joined him. "If you lean out far enough over the railing, you can see the lake. When I have enough time to get there, I like to run on the lake path. Being near the water invigorates me."

"Me, too. It kind of renews my spirit when I'm flagging."

They exchanged an understanding smile.

Something inside Megan shifted, coiled in a way that would have been tension if it hadn't felt warm.

Speaking of warmth…

"Have a seat by the fire and dry off." She indicated the sofa closest to the radiating fireplace. "I'll get some coffee, unless you'd prefer tea or cocoa."

"Coffee's good. Thanks." He settled on the sofa.

It looked half its original size with him seated there instead of her or Amber, the ruffled and beaded throw pillows Amber loved making him look like a giant dropped into a princess's palace.

Grinning to herself, Megan trotted to her room to change out of her soaked clothes, not having had on as sensible a hoodie as Jack, and then walked into the kitchen. Amber was already there, having changed into dry clothes herself, and scooping ground coffee into the filter.

"Did you leave him with the fire?" Amber asked.

"I did." Megan took milk from the refrigerator to heat. "He looks exhausted."

"I don't think he got any sleep last night. I mean, by the time he got to the southside and back here, he didn't have time." Amber pulled mugs from the cabinet over the coffee maker. "Do you like him?"

"What a silly question. I don't know him."

"Hmm." Amber grinned and glanced toward Tess, who was sidling up to the table, where a few toast crumbs had landed on the floor earlier. "Go lie down, Tess."

Tess halted as though she had brakes, cast Amber a guilty look, and padded from the room on soft, furry paws.

Megan laughed. "The look on her face. She can never figure out how you know what she's up to."

"She forgets I can hear her. What is it this time, crumbs?"

"From breakfast. I'll get the broom. No sense tempting the poor thing."

Megan swept the kitchen floor, thinking she needed to be a better housekeeper or get one of those robot vacuums. Though Amber brushed her every day, Tess shed like crazy. Plus, Megan tended to leave notes to herself scattered over every surface, and Amber was good at cooking, but not necessarily at cleaning up afterward.

By the time she finished sweeping, the coffee maker had beeped. She set it and warm milk and sugar on a tray. Amber followed with another tray of cups, and they headed for the living room. "Shh." She halted herself and Amber in the doorway.

Across the room, Jack slumped in the corner of the sofa, Tess sprawled across his feet like a pair of giant, fuzzy slippers. Neither of them moved at Megan and Amber's approach.

"They're asleep," Megan murmured.

"Then let's leave them." Amber turned back to the kitchen.

They went into the sunroom they used as a home office and turned on the space heaters beneath their desks. "I have a thousand phone calls to make," Megan said. She set her phone on the charger and popped a set of Bluetooth headphones with a mic over her ears.

She hadn't yet heard from Gary or his wife, Janet, and that concerned her. Maybe he was hurt worse than she had at first thought. She dialed her phone to try to reach Janet, but just reached the voice mail. She'd have to try again later.

Megan had been a licensed PI for three years, and still felt incompetent at handling her own life at times. Her work was her life. Other than running along the lake, she did nothing much else for fun. She worked. Even at home she worked. Her desk was a testimony to that. All that was missing was her laptop.

She had made a dozen phone calls and felt as though she had left two dozen voicemail messages. Insurance company. Arranging for copies of police reports on her car and computer having been stolen and for copies of the fire report so she could make insurance claims. Cleaning up and inspecting the office.

She wished she were curled up on the sofa across from Jack and napping by the fire herself.

"Why do I think I can run the office?" she asked aloud. "I can't think which phone call I should follow up on first. Doesn't anyone return messages these days?"

"What are they?" Amber popped up the lid of her laptop.

"Enter your password," a synthesized female voice that wasn't at all monotone said.

"I can help make some of them, I'm sure." Amber plugged in her own headphones and began to type twice as fast as Megan could. "Like all the things having to do with the office and insurance. It's my job, after all."

"I know, but..." Megan began to write on a sticky note. "I want to be the boss. That means it's all my responsibility."

"Gary never did everything on his own. He had Janet until she decided she wanted to retire and they hired me." Amber cast Megan a warm smile. "I like my job. I'm not about to leave you. And you can always ask Jack to stay and help."

"Don't be ridiculous," Megan said a little sharper than she intended. "He has big things going for his future.

After this week, he'll want out of here as fast as he can get."

And leave her behind?

The idea made Megan feel a little queasy and definitely sad for reasons she wasn't about to examine. She couldn't consider being attracted to a man who was leaving town soon, not when she was trying to stay alive.

Jack woke feeling oddly refreshed for having slept only three hours in the past thirty-six and having a slightly stiff neck from slumping in the corner of a sofa. His feet were nearly too warm beneath a furry weight, and someone had laid a fluffy blanket over him.

The furry weight must have been watching him, for the moment Jack opened his eyes, the golden retriever leaped to her feet and began to lavish him with puppy kisses, tail wagging dangerously close to the gas fireplace someone had turned to low.

"Tess, no," a soft voice called from the doorway.

"It's all right," Jack said. "I'm awake."

"I hope she didn't wake you." Amber came into the room patting her leg. "Tess, come."

The dog raced across the room to take up position beside her person.

"Good girl." Amber rubbed the furry ears, then glanced to Jack. "Do you need coffee now?"

"I should go home. I didn't mean to sleep." At the sight of Megan coming down the hallway behind Amber, Jack felt heat rise into his face. "Your couch is too comfortable."

"We know." Megan's smile was warm. "But you can't go home. We have work to do." Her cheeks reddened, as well. "I mean, you can't go home yet. It's not like we're holding you hostage or anything."

Jack grinned at her. "I thought maybe I'd outlived my welcome."

"Oh, I don't think so." Amber winked and turned sideways to move around Megan. "I'm ordering pizza. Food always makes work go faster. Chicago-style?"

"Is there anything else worth eating?" Jack rose, muscles tightening the longer he remained in one position. "Mind if I get some fresh air on your balcony?"

"Of course not." For a moment, Megan looked as though she might join him, then she murmured something about helping Amber and retreated.

Jack stepped into air far colder than it had been that morning, though the rain had stopped. Someone nearby had a wood-burning fireplace they'd started up to scent the air. In the street, bicyclists vied with cars for the right of way. Shouts and honking horns seemed a long way down.

They *were* a long way down. At least forty feet. Jack tested the railing for security. It was solid and a good four feet high.

Awake and sure the sooner he and Megan figured out what they should do next, the better, he returned to the apartment and found Megan setting the table in the dining room.

"Coffee?" she asked.

"Thanks. Black will do."

"Have a seat." She waved him to a chair and disappeared into the kitchen.

Jack looked out the window instead. It, too, was high up, of course. From what he'd seen, only their door was vulnerable to intrusion.

But why would anyone want to intrude? Why had someone tried to abduct Megan after smoking her and the others out of the office? Why had someone tried to push him off the train and tampered with his gas meter?

Jack had only one answer, and he didn't like it.

"So they want us dead," he said to Megan when she brought in a mug of steaming coffee for him. "Because we know exactly what?"

"We saw that man do something that made Cahill appear dead. No one we know has been able to identify him, but we would if we spotted him," Megan said.

"Except we saw her alive not a half hour later."

"We have this on video," Megan said. "True, his body blocks sight of what he did to Cahill to make her fall and remain still for so long, but we have a pretty clear look at his face and him holding a gun." She touched his arm. "You have evidence he shot at us."

"I have evidence that I was hurt." Jack covered the place on his bicep where Megan's fingers had grazed, as though he could hold that gentleness to him. "No proof it was any particular kind of weapon."

"It's just giving me a particular kind of headache." Megan rubbed her temples. "Or maybe I'm just tired."

"And hungry." Amber pulled her phone from her pocket. "Pizza will be here in two minutes. Do we make the delivery person bring it to us?"

"I'll get it." Jack thought the long walk down and back up again would do him good, maybe finish the job of making his brain work since the caffeine hadn't yet jolted it into action.

He smelled the rich tang of tomato sauce, spicy sausage and melted cheese in a thick, buttery crust the instant he opened the building door. The box was large and relatively heavy, and he ran it back upstairs, happy when he wasn't winded at the top. The slight lightheadedness of running up three flights of steps on a nearly empty stomach, while smelling some of the best aromas he knew, gave him a clarity he'd been seeking all day.

"The answer's clear." He set the pizza box on the table. "I need to retrace our steps from last night, starting at the tree."

"And what if they are there waiting for us?" Megan asked.

"If we don't draw them out," Jack said, "we'll be running looking over our shoulders until they stop us." He cleared his throat. "Until they succeed in killing us."

NINE

Megan and Amber took a rideshare to the home of one of their coworkers. She lived in the northwest part of the city, a lovely neighborhood near a forest preserve, where many of the city's police lived. Melissa—Mel to those who knew better—was the daughter of two cops but had chosen the PI route instead of going to the academy herself. If anyone was capable of ensuring Amber and Tess weren't assaulted because of their closeness to Megan, that person was Mel. She lived in the same one-and-a-half-story home she'd lived in all her life, now too big for one person with her parents retired and moved south, and her younger sister married and in the suburbs.

"But what about you?" Mel asked Megan.

"I can take care of myself." She glanced at Amber. "I'm sorry if that offends your independence, but you'd have a harder time getting away from someone who meant you harm."

Amber bowed her head. "Or seeing him coming until he's too close for running to do me any good. The best I can hope for is that Tess would lick him to death."

The ridiculous suggestion made them all laugh.

"Be careful." Mel's gray-green eyes darkened with concern.

"I don't think this bad guy is the only thing she has to be careful of." Amber grinned. "Jack sounds pretty attractive."

Mel raised her eyebrows. "Oh?"

"Yeah, sure, he's good-looking." Megan knew she had put on the "guess I noticed" attitude a little too strongly.

Mel and Amber laughed.

Megan hefted her messenger bag over her shoulder. "I need to get going."

"Is your cell phone charged fully?" Amber asked.

"Do you have bullets?" Mel added.

"Yes, and no." Megan opened the front door. "I never carry a gun. You know that."

"What's the point in having a carry license—"

Megan slipped outside before Mel finished her sentence.

The argument was old and tired. Mel didn't see the point in not being armed. Megan didn't see the point in being armed. Megan had always used the excuse that her cases weren't anything one got killed over.

First time for everything.

She could go without some firsts—like getting chased down by a murderer. Or would-be murderer.

And she and Jack thought they could find out who it was before he killed them.

She had always believed herself good at her job. She had ferreted out some amazingly small details that had solved cases—a wife who swore her husband was hiding money from her, a missing sixteen-year-old girl, even a lost piece of jewelry once upon a time. She had no idea how to go about seeking a man who seemed to want her dead, a man the cops didn't believe was the same person who had perpetrated all the crimes.

And she had no idea why Jack thought he would have

the right skills, either. He might be a super accountant, but dealing with deep records and balancing reconciliation were highly different animals. Actually, one was an animal and the other, the one with which Jack was the most familiar, was concrete numbers that didn't change their symbolism, just their values when added, subtracted or divided.

Maybe he had learned a thing or two from his cop uncle. Or maybe his father had been a cop, too. She had no idea. She knew very little about him. Yet she trusted him enough to meet him in the evening in a potentially dangerous situation.

She trusted him because comments he'd made, the way he treated his sister and others whom he met, told her they shared the same values, the same beliefs. His confidence without arrogance told her he was trustworthy. She prided herself on her ability to make accurate judgments about people within a few hours of meeting them. She had honed the ability. It helped in the execution of her job.

She wouldn't have a job if she didn't put this matter to rest. The agency couldn't continue with its agents being threatened or hurt. No way would Megan be responsible for the harm to others. Gary's bout of smoke inhalation and mild concussion was bad enough.

Megan exited the bus at the train station and caught the next L to downtown. They were meeting in the Loop, the area of downtown surrounded by the L tracks overhead, the heart of the city. Two of the lines moved underground there, so Jack and Megan could meet out in the open, within sight of security guards and service agents for the transit authority. The worst part for Megan was the tunnel between one train line and another. The hour was early enough that shoppers and those coming into town for dinner or the theater filled the space, yet crowds almost felt worse than being alone. Following someone without them noticing was much harder in open spaces or sparsely populated areas.

She slithered close to the wall so she only had to keep watch on one side with an occasional look back. People had been shot in the tunnel during the rush hour. They had been stabbed, too. Mostly over drug deals gone wrong or some kind of gang violence. Getting away with it, melting back into the crowd was easy. A run up a flight of steps and the perpetrator disappeared onto the street, through a building with more than one entrance and exit, or down an alley and into another L station.

By the time she reached the platform for the train going back into Lincoln Park, Megan's heart was racing, her stomach knotting. She spotted danger in every woman with blond hair or man with thick eyebrows.

"I'm the hunter, not the hunted," she told herself, not realizing she'd spoken aloud until people began to stare at her and give her a wide birth. Since this let her know if anyone got too close, she repeated the words out loud again.

By the time she reached Jack, she was close to laughing.

"I'm glad you think this job is amusing." He sounded grumpy, but his blue eyes twinkled. "Can I get in on the joke?"

"Sure. Later. Ready to turn into a sardine on the next train?"

They crossed the platform with thousands of others, allowed two trains to pass before one approached that was only halfway full—at least empty enough they found seats side by side.

Seats so small and close together her shoulder kept

bumping into Jack's arm. His left, fortunately. He still seemed to favor his right one, holding it a little stiffly, despite assuring her it was just fine.

"So tell me what you were laughing about," Jack said after they rode together in silence for at least five minutes.

She took a deep breath. Above the aroma of someone's take-home dinner set on the bench beside her, Megan caught a whiff of Jack's scent. Something clean and refreshing, a kind of minty scent, but not peppermint or anything so strong. She feared she still smelled of smoke, having changed her clothes, but not having had the time to wash her hair since being in the office. The smell wasn't pleasant like wood smoke. It was a chemical sting. Would tugging her hair into a messy knot make the stench less noticeable, or worse?

"You were saying?" Jack prompted.

She told him. He laughed, then turned serious.

"Have you thought much about what we're going to do first?"

"Walk from where I parked my car the second time to Cahill's house," Megan said.

"What do you think we'll find?"

She shrugged. "Bullet casings? People who might have seen or heard something from inside their apartments?"

"If you do that," Jack said, "I'll go look behind the Cahill house."

"Alone?"

"I'd rather do it alone than drag you into it."

"Like you're more qualified than I am." She snorted.

The train drew into a station, and the car emptied. Jack stretched his long legs into the aisle, tapping his toes on the opposite seat before drawing his legs in again and resting his elbows on his knees. "I am more qualified." He looked at the gritty floor. "I used to be a cop."

* * *

He had known her for not quite a day, and already he was telling her something he hadn't told a new acquaintance since… Well, since one had to be a new acquaintance not to know. She was just too comfortable to be around.

At the moment, a quick glance at her face told him she wasn't comfortable at all. She looked taut enough to knock down with a breath. He might have been mistaken but he believed she moved away from him a few inches.

"How long?" she demanded. "I mean, when? I mean… Is you not being one any longer the reason why you and your uncle—never mind. None of my business." She raised her hands as though erecting a barrier between them.

"I don't know. Maybe it is your business." Jack straightened and prepared to exit at the next station.

He waited for Megan to go ahead of him, then followed her down the platform to the escalator. Her back was stiff, her ponytail practically bristling. He grinned. Even when he knew what they were doing was likely to get them nowhere but into trouble—the dangerous kind—she made him smile.

She had a right to be angry with him, he supposed. She knew more about Grace than she did about him. Yet she seemed to trust him.

Probably for the same reasons he trusted her—they shared values. The ones they cared about came first.

At the top of the escalator, they stopped at a coffee shop and grabbed coffee by silent agreement, then sat in the chilly evening air with the electronics store glowing like a space station on one side and endless traffic on the other. They could watch everyone going by yet be secure from anyone trying to harm them. No one would, with those huge, plate glass windows lit up beside them.

"Spill," Megan said.

"I went to two years of college, then entered the academy. Police academy. My uncle got me onto the force right away, and I started work when I was barely twenty-one." Jack hid his emotions over the time period behind an expressionless tone and coffee steam. "I lasted six months. I was in a good neighborhood, so didn't see much violence. Catching kids doing drugs, traffic tickets. I was bored to death, frankly. So my uncle decided to send me out with an experienced officer on a domestic violence call. He shouldn't have. But he wanted me to see real work and the good we could do in fraught circumstances."

He sipped and scanned the square, watched people getting on and off buses, and admired a fancy sports car cruising to the corner—anything to avoid watching Megan's face.

"It didn't go well?" she prompted.

"You could say so." He barked a humorless laugh. "It was a nice high-rise building. Not the sort of place one expects screaming fights and violence. But the husband had lost his job and was out of his head drunk. My temporary partner tried to calm him down." Jack swallowed. "And got stabbed with the neck of a broken bottle."

Megan gasped, her face whitening. "Did he… Is he okay?"

"Eventually. I'll spare you the details. Let's just say his career was over, and so was mine. I couldn't imagine putting myself through that kind of a scene again. I thought if I'd been more experienced, I would have known what to do. But I was useless, and my uncle was demoted for sending me out instead of the man's regular partner. They all looked at me like it was my fault."

"So you left."

"I left and went back to school."

"Yet you want to be an FBI agent?" Megan looked confused.

"An accountant for the FBI, possibly the most boring, stable job in the whole agency. I won't be in the field. I'll be safe so Grace doesn't have to worry about me coming home at night."

Megan drew a design with her thumbnail on the side of her cup, concentrating as though she created an important work of art in the thermoplastic, before she raised her head and asked, "So what were you doing in that tree with me last night?"

"It was supposed to be harmless observation," Jack began, then realized he should tell her the entire truth. "And your boss sent me there to look after you."

Even before he finished speaking, Megan had shoved back her chair so hard it slammed into an empty table behind her. "Gary would never do that to me. He knows I'm capable of taking care of myself. And why would he send you anyway?"

Ignoring the number of people staring at them, Jack rose and carried his empty cup to the trash. Megan's running shoes thudded behind him. He didn't glance back at her.

"Are you walking away?" she demanded.

"I'm a coward. I'm getting out of the line of fire." He tried to lighten the mood.

And failed.

Megan's cup arced past him for a perfect shot into the trash receptacle. "Jack Luskie, talk to me." Her voice was quiet now.

He thought quiet might be dangerous with her.

He faced her. "I knew who you were and where to find you."

"You did." She sighed. "You knew way too much about

my case for my liking at the time." She set her hands on her hips. "But how did Gary know about you?"

"Cahill's company told him they'd hired me to go over their accounts to look for where the embezzlement happened and how."

"But why wouldn't Gary trust me?" She blinked, and a droplet of water sparkled on her cheek.

Jack caught it on the pad of his thumb. "You'll have to ask him."

Women's tears didn't bother Jack, as in he didn't want to run from them. What bothered him was the depth of hurt Megan's single tear displayed. He understood. He had been betrayed by someone he respected, too.

"If it's any consolation," Jack told her in a quiet voice, "I think Gary was wrong. I think you would have done just fine last night if you'd been on your own."

"I wouldn't have fallen out of the tree on my own," she shot back.

Jack laughed. "You're probably right. Should we get to work now before everyone's tucked in for the night?"

She nodded and headed for the corner.

Once they had reached the other side of the busy intersection and headed into a quieter, more residential area, Megan asked, "Do you think risking our safety doing this will do any good?"

"I have no idea. I just know we can't sit back and wait for one of us to get killed before we can feel safe going about our business."

"Don't you think Cahill and whoever is working with her will give up on us and move on someplace safe? I mean, they stole a great deal of money. Surely they're better off in Grand Cayman or something."

"You'd think." Jack scanned the side street they were about to turn onto. It was the street where Megan had parked her car the second time. "But some people don't like leaving loose ends."

"Like witnesses."

"Like witnesses."

But they looked for witnesses of any kind they could find. On a Saturday night, people thronged the sidewalks. Even the side streets held their share of groups off to dinner or other entertainment. They tried to catch people walking out of buildings past which he and Megan had run the night before, presuming those people lived in the area and might have been at home.

A few remembered hearing gunfire. Like sensible city dwellers, they ignored the ruckus and stayed away from the windows. No one had seen anything, not Jack and Megan running, not anyone chasing them. No one had seen someone stealing Megan's car or even hearing the alarm go off.

"If my hair didn't still smell like chemical smoke," Megan said after a fruitless two hours, "I'd think we made this all up."

"Not to mention your video." Jack couldn't resist tucking an errant curl behind her ear.

He didn't think her hair smelled like smoke of any kind. She smelled more like autumn leaves to him—crisp and somewhere between sweet and spicy.

"The cops are right." Megan leaned against the trunk of an elm. "That video is next to useless."

"Next to, but not useless." Finding himself gazing at her, Jack forced his eyes away and realized they stood at the entrance to the alley leading behind Cahill's house. He craned his neck to see the handful of houses between them and the Cahill bungalow. It was dark. The garage door stood open but appeared empty of vehicles. He wanted a closer look. He didn't want Megan with him when he got a closer look. At the same time, he wasn't leaving her there alone at the corner of the alley.

"Want to revisit the tree?" he asked.

She gave him a look that said he had gone too long without enough sleep. "I think I'd rather have a trip to the dentist."

"Let's walk up here and see what we can, though." Jack moved around her so he walked between her and the houses on the Cahill side.

The garage was indeed empty of vehicles. An overhead light showed the usual contents like shovels and rakes and cans of paint, but not so much as a bicycle tire spoke of a mode of transportation having been there.

"Strange to leave the door open and the light on," Megan whispered.

"Unless they're coming right back." Jack moved past the garage.

The gate to the backyard was also open. A bed pillow lay on the walkway around the garage, its feather stuffing drifting around like snow. A pillow was the sort of thing that might fall from overly burdened arms as someone raced to pack a car…

Or van. A van like the one that had followed them the night before.

Increasingly uneasy, Jack started along the walkway.

"Don't go into the yard," Megan whispered from the alley. "It could be a trap to lure you in."

She was right. Cahill and company might be trying to lure him and Megan into their orbit. Yet they wouldn't have known the two of them were coming. And this was rather an elaborate trap to be set up at the last moment.

"I don't think anyone's here," Jack said. "But I'll check. Wait there in the alley. In fact, close the gate."

She didn't follow him. Neither did she close the gate.

Jack felt her gaze upon him as he traversed the short sidewalk along the garage and swished through the grass. Once he reached the bottom of the steps to the deck, the back door had come into view. The open back door. A single overhead light shone on the polished wood floor of a breakfast room…and more.

He could be mistaken, but he was almost positive there was a body on the floor. He might be seeing another fallen pillow, a frill of dropped fabric. A lost sofa cushion.

His footfalls ringing hollowly on the wooden planks, he crossed the deck to stand in the doorway.

He hadn't been mistaken. He and Megan hadn't been mistaken the night before. The cops could say the video was too dark and obscure for any conclusive evidence, but they couldn't dismiss this.

Not the youngest rookie on the force could dismiss the body lying on the floor, sheltered from the open door by a table and chairs, only her legs sticking out in plain sight—legs wrapped in the same gauzy blue dress she'd worn the night before. The man must have dragged her inside after killing her on the deck.

"Megan," Jack spoke as softly yet clearly as he could so she would hear him from where she stood in the alley, "get moving away from here."

"Not without you." She took a step toward him, the flashlight on her phone a bright eye in the darkness around her. "I'm not leaving—"

"It's a trap," he shouted.

He didn't know how or where, just knew no one left a door open with a dead body inside without a truly good reason. Trapping two people he had already tried to kill would be a truly good reason to the killer of the woman inside.

Jack tripped on the threshold. It shuddered beneath his feet. A weakness in an old house, or a trigger?

He kept backing away, his gaze on the body, the table, the doorway. He saw no wires to indicate an explosive, no movement to indicate a shooter taking aim. The area was shockingly silent, so silent his footfalls on the deck planks sounded like thunder, like branches creaking in a high wind.

No, not his footfalls. The branches were creaking, casting shadows in the light from the house and his phone flashlight. Yet the night was still, part of the silence.

"Jack, run," Megan cried. "The tree—"

A thunderous roar drowned Megan's scream. The tree trunk was fine, as straight and solid as ever. The branches were not. Something large and dark was sliding off the roof and into the tree, weighing down the limbs, snapping them off like toothpicks and sliding straight for Jack's head.

TEN

Megan felt helpless. If she ran toward Jack, she would get hurt herself, possibly killed. If she didn't help him, he would most certainly die. She took the only other action presented to her.

She entered the yard, grabbed the heavy wrought iron table from the deck and shoved it in Jack's direction. It screeched across the boards of the deck. Useless. She managed to lift a matching chair and throw it. Her missiles blocked Jack from her sight, but she heard his shout, then the metallic rumble of rock striking iron. Fireflies of sparks flew into the night, and the bass rumbled on and on and on, fading beneath Megan's shouting of Jack's name.

"Here." His voice was winded, but clear and very much alive. "I'm here." He moved then, creeping from beneath the twisted mess of table and chairs.

"Are you all right?" Megan ran to him and dropped to her knees beside his still prone figure. "Did you get hit?"

"Not much. The table stopped it." Jack pushed himself to a sitting position. He glanced from the table to Megan. "How did you manage to move that thing so far so fast?"

Megan shrugged. "The strength of adrenaline?"

"That was...something." He still sounded breathless.

She rested one hand on his shoulder. “Are you sure you’re all right? Should I call an ambulance?”

“No, but we’re going to have to call the cops. That was a trap set deliberately.”

“For us?”

“Or anyone who got too close.”

Megan shook her head. “How would they have had time?”

“It might have been here for a while to keep people from the house. Step on the threshold and…mashed potatoes.”

Megan coughed. “Thanks for that image.”

“Well, see what you think of this image.” He closed his eyes as though he pondered something new. “Explaining what we’re doing here to the cops.”

“Ms. O’Clare, do you always attract trouble?” inquired Sergeant Dave Luskie.

Megan gave Jack’s uncle a blank stare. If she answered that question, she would concede that she caused trouble at any time. Concede she would not. She had not attracted this trouble. It had found her. She had been happy to turn the matter of Cahill over to the police and let it go. But when someone caused trouble for her and her friends, not to mention her place of employment, she had no hesitation in running the criminals down herself.

“I didn’t find the body,” Megan answered at last. “I wasn’t anywhere near the house.”

“You were in the alley behind the house,” Luskie said.

“An alley is public property.” Megan smiled.

She could be respectful without giving in to any of the scenarios he had tried to form around her escapade with Jack. She just wished he felt the same way. His dislike of his nephew seemed to spill over onto her.

"You opened the gate," Luskie said. "That could be considered trespass."

"The gate was open."

"So you say."

"We never touched the gate. Fingerprint analysis will prove that to be true."

She had been fingerprinted for the PI license.

"Gloves. You both know enough to wear gloves when breaking and entering."

Megan gripped the edge of the scarred table in the police station interview room. She would not give in to the stereotype that redheads had fiery tempers. She rarely lost hers. But being accused, however obliquely, that she was lying was something that set up her hackles and threatened to provoke her into doing something she always regretted immediately, such as leaping to her feet and shouting that she would not have her integrity questioned. Her mother would have added that an O'Clare was not a liar. Maybe they weren't, but they knew how to twist the truth.

And because her mother chose to say something so ridiculous, something that sounded more like it should come from the mouth of a Victorian duchess than an attorney with political ambitions, Megan avoided ever using her family name or connections to promote herself in any way. She was who she was—smart, reliable, honest. If Jack's uncle chose not to believe her, declaring otherwise would not change his mind.

She dropped her hands to her lap. "I have nothing else to report, sir. If you think you have reason to hold me, I can't stop you. I will, however, have to have an attorney before I say anything else."

"Do you have reason to say anything else?" Luskie demanded.

Megan said nothing.

Luskie sighed and walked from the room. He didn't go far. Through the door, she heard him speaking on his phone. Just the rumble of his voice, not the words.

She had no idea what they had done with Jack. She suspected he sat in a room similar to hers, with someone else questioning him. He would be calm, Megan expected, and his story would be the same as hers. It had to be, unless he twisted or stretched the truth.

She didn't think he would. He was honest.

His story wouldn't be exactly the same. He had gone into the yard because of the open rear door, and he had found the body.

A body. Cahill, for sure, lying on the kitchen floor like a discarded and broken doll.

Jack had taken pictures. He hadn't wanted Megan to see them, but she had looked anyway. She needed to grow immune to grizzly sights like dead bodies. Investigators didn't find them often, but it was not unheard of.

With her, it wasn't heard of at all. Or it hadn't been until that night. Or had that been last night? But if Cahill had been dead the night before, who had been with the man who chased them?

Megan sighed and speared her fingers through her hair. Her ponytail band popped, flying across the room, useless. Her hair tumbled around her shoulders, out of control from getting rain-soaked earlier. She dug through her bag, seeking another band. She almost always carried extras with her.

No band. Not so much as a bobby pin.

Hearing Luskie end his phone call, Megan straightened in her chair and tucked her hair behind her ears. When he reentered the room, she sat straight, but relaxed, hands folded in her lap. All those lessons in comportment her mother sent her to were coming in handy. Little had her mother known Megan would realize how important they were while she was in a police interview room after being interrogated over a murder. Over a murder she and Jack had probably witnessed after all.

She hadn't been mistaken the night before. However much she wished she were wrong, the killing had taken place. The police would take them seriously now.

She didn't wait for Luskie to return to his seat before attacking with her own inquiry. "Will you and your brothers in blue decide Jack and I weren't exaggerating about last night, Sergeant Luskie, sir?"

"We will take another look into things." He gripped the back of his chair. "The video wasn't conclusive enough, and since we can only presume what you saw wasn't any better than the video, your testimony wasn't much good, either. But now we have a body..."

"Which you didn't find when you searched last night?" Megan prompted.

Luskie stared at a point over Megan's head—a camera maybe? "We didn't have a warrant to search and not enough evidence to get one."

"But now?"

"What we conclude about last night will depend on what time an autopsy says the deceased died."

That made sense. If she had been gone four hours or twenty-four, the autopsy would say, and Megan and Jack would know.

"So you believe someone has been trying to harm us?" Megan couldn't bring herself to say "trying to murder us."

"If the deceased died last night, then maybe you have a point."

Megan gritted her teeth.

"Until we have more information," Luskie continued,

"take ordinary precautions when you move about the city, and stay off social media. You might want to ditch your cell phones altogether."

Because they could be traced through their cell phones if someone had managed to grab access.

"The beautiful people can simply get new phones. I'm sure that's no hardship for you, either, Miss O'Clare."

Actually, it was a hardship. Her parents had cut off her allowance when she got her PI license and chose to practice. Though she knew they would come to her aid in any emergency, the cost would be her agreeing to giving up her practice and going back to school.

The mere idea of it made her sick. She'd be better suited to becoming a doctor if she kept finding bodies and got used to them.

Luskie rounded the table and stood behind Megan as though he were about to pull out her chair. "Get back to chasing lost dogs and straying husbands, Ms. O'Clare, and leave police work to us. You're safer that way."

"Only if someone isn't trying to kill me." Afraid he might be about to pat her on her head, Megan rose before he could pull out her chair. "Then I'm free to go."

"You are, but not too far." He tried to stride past her, but the space wasn't large enough. "We will probably have more questions."

Megan whipped open a door. "I'll be where I'm safe."

But at that moment, she didn't know where safe was.

Jack needed a decent night's sleep. He needed a shower and clean clothes and time to recharge his spirit and mind. But he couldn't go home. His house was probably not safe, even with the explosive device deactivated.

And what of Megan? He couldn't send her alone home to that empty apartment. He especially couldn't send her to that house where Amber had gone. Not by public transit. Not this late at night on her own, even in a taxi. That left one viable solution.

He didn't want to take it. Conceding that Grace was better off with her relatives than at home at present was one thing. Asking for himself was quite another. It was asking a favor. They wanted Grace around. They didn't want Jack.

No, that wasn't quite right. Jack didn't want to owe his aunt and uncle a favor. He wanted to prove to them he was self-reliant. They needed to see he wasn't that rookie cop who couldn't cut the job. He could have cut it—if it weren't for his uncle endangering someone to teach his nephew a lesson. He had a great future ahead of him. He could provide Grace with a great future, too.

Far away from Megan.

He shook that thought out of his head. His life had nothing to do with Megan once they got through this crisis. Their futures ran in different directions, directions as divergent as their pasts had been. Right now, this time when they were thrown together was to teach them some lesson.

Leaving the interview room and seeing his uncle in the corridor with Megan, Jack feared he understood at least what some of that lesson might be.

The time had come for him to let past mistakes go. His uncle had surely paid in his heart for his choices where Jack was concerned. Dave Luskie was a good man, had always been a good and honest cop, from all reports. He'd been demoted for the error he made with Jack, and had worked hard to regain his reputation, getting wounded in the process.

That his uncle wanted to take custody of Grace away from Jack was a wholly different matter, one to be resolved at another time if necessary. For the moment, Jack needed to remember, needed to convince himself, that family was family and helped one another in times of crisis.

This was a time of crisis if ever one existed.

He headed down the hallway to meet up with Megan and his uncle.

"You look tired," Megan said with a smile. "Did they use the thumbscrews?"

"I feel more like they used them on my eyeballs." Jack rubbed eyes he was sure must be as red as Megan's hair. "I've had three hours of sleep since yesterday morning."

"Then you'd better go home and get more," Uncle Dave said.

"About that." Jack's mouth was suddenly dry. He found himself wanting to shuffle his feet and play with the detritus of change and keys in his pants pockets, while avoiding everyone's gaze. He was fifteen again and asking his uncle if he'd come to the school career day fair and talk about being a cop.

The last time he'd asked Dave for a favor? Must have been. Jack's dad had still been alive, a detective with CPD and embroiled in a case that wouldn't let him go long enough to keep his promise about filling in the role at the fair.

Uncle Dave had said of course he'd do it and had laughed at Jack's nervousness. "I learned my lesson with my own boys," he had said. "I can only hope to make up for it with you."

Jack hadn't understood those words at the time. He hadn't thought about them until now, when he needed another favor.

Megan and Dave were staring at Jack with identical quizzical expressions.

Jack cleared his throat. "Do you think Megan and I could crash at your place tonight? We'd be safest there… If it isn't too much trouble…"

His uncle's eyes widened. His lips parted, but he said nothing for several moments.

Beside him, Megan began to speak, then pressed her fingers to her lips as though making herself be quiet.

"If it would put out Aunt Julie too much—" Jack began.

"No, not at all." Dave turned away abruptly. "I'll give her a call, and I'll have someone drive you over there." He pulled his cell phone from his pocket and tapped the screen, while strolling down the hall.

"I can go to Mel's house," Megan said.

"Do you think you should?" Jack asked. "I mean, this man could have left town, but I'm not sure he did. Everything was too staged. The open doors. The lights left on. The dropped pillow—those are all signs of a hasty departure."

"But who takes a feather pillow, then drops it when one is running away?" Megan fiddled with the zipper tab on her jacket. "I should have realized that right away. If the pillow is important enough to take in the first place, one isn't going to leave it behind." Her fidgeting fingers moved to her hair, her glorious red hair spilling around her shoulders for the first time since he'd met her.

She was always pretty. At that moment, despite dark circles beneath her eyes, she looked beautiful to Jack.

And he needed to get his mind away from such thinking. They were strangers thrown together under extraordinary circumstances. Nothing more. Ever.

"That's why we need sleep," Jack said. "One doesn't notice the obvious and thinks absurd thoughts when one hasn't had enough sleep."

"Thank you for thinking about that." Megan shoved

her hands into her coat pockets. "Do your aunt and uncle have enough room? I mean, Mel's house is pretty small."

"They have a good-sized condo in a high-rise along Lake Shore Drive."

Megan shot him a questioning glance.

"My aunt is in sales. High-end clothes and jewelry."

"So why—" She shook her head. "None of my business."

"Why does he still work and at night?" Jack supplied the question for her. "He could have retired a couple years ago but feels the need to make up for the mistake with me."

"Sounds like all of you need a little forgiving to go on—you of him and he of himself." Megan's voice was soft, barely above a murmur. After she said her piece, she ducked her head. "Like I have a right to talk that way."

"Yeah, well, it's always easier to see other people's flaws than our own." Since her hair hid her face now that a band no longer held the curls back, Jack brushed back the thick strands. They were soft, like some fancy yarn his mother had once used to knit a sweater for Grace. "Helps to recognize our flaws."

Megan nodded and tucked her hair behind her ears. She appeared as though she were about to say something, but Dave paced toward them, phone still in his hand.

"Julie says for you two to come on over. Miss O'Clare can bunk with Grace in the guest room, and you can have the sofa bed in Julie's office."

As much as he wanted to sleep for a week, Jack hoped he would be awake in time for the sunrise. He hoped the clouds would blow away and they could see the sunrise over the lake. He didn't know if he had witnessed anything more beautiful.

"We're ready to go," Dave called to them. "Go out back. There'll be a car waiting for you."

"Thanks." Jack held out his hand.

Uncle Dave shook it. "Happy to help." His voice was rough, like he had a need for a glass of water.

Feeling a little the same way, Jack offered his arm to Megan, as though they were striding up a red carpet instead of the slightly grimy halls of a police station, and left the building. As promised, a car awaited them. Since only one of them could sit in front, they opted to both sit in the back, like prisoners.

"Are you sure this is all right?" Megan whispered once the doors closed them in.

Locked them in.

In moments, they were on their way for the mile-long ride to the condo that overlooked Lake Michigan.

Jack glanced at the young patrolman driving. He had his dispatch radio on but might still be able to hear.

"Of course it's all right. I think—" He paused to clear his throat. "I think me asking actually made him happy."

"Absolutely."

"Why are you so sure?"

"I can see his face without your bias."

Jack nodded, then couldn't resist. "Wonder if I'd see the same with your family."

"Not likely." Megan wrinkled her nose. "They don't show emotion."

"With a name like O'Clare?"

"Don't stereotype us. Or them, anyway. I left when I was eighteen and haven't gone back."

"With them only—what?—ten miles away?"

Megan shrugged. "Ten miles. Ten thousand miles. It's all the same when one leaves the nest."

She sounded so distressed he wanted to reach out and

take her hand in his, offer her comfort. He could say words, a lot of them, words about reaching out to them and forgiving them for their stubbornness and maybe examining her own willful attitude about going her own way. He said nothing. She was a smart lady. She likely knew all the responses already and wouldn't welcome him saying them aloud.

"So what do we do tomorrow?" Megan asked in an abrupt change of subject.

"Go on about our business, I suppose. With a body in the picture, the cops will take this seriously."

"But not our protection."

"That's a different matter. One I haven't figured out yet."

They stopped talking, and the car pulled into a circular drive before a tall, elegant building across the highway that ran along the lake. On one side, headlights, taillights and brake lights flickered past like a galaxy of stars running at warp speed. On the other, more light ran up and up and up like a constellation, or maybe a spaceship racing toward—what? Destruction? A bright and lovely future? Beyond the road, the lake stretched black and infinite in the darkness, only an occasional whitecap whipped up by the wind there to remind them winter was on its way.

Jack prayed for the bright future. He needed good news. He needed rest. He needed reassurance the next hour wasn't going to be a disaster of accusations.

As though she read his mind, Megan tucked her hand into his and squeezed his fingers. "I doubt your aunt bites."

"Nope, but she can bark your ears off." Jack returned Megan's finger hug and headed for the revolving doors on the front of the building.

Once they were beyond the glass barricade, the air

turned warm. Thick carpet deadened the sound of their footfalls. A doorman stopped them to request ID and destination.

"Go on up." The man gave them both a steely glare. "She's expecting you, and I never forget a face."

"Good for you." Megan's tone held just a hint of snark.

Jack didn't blame her. Just because they appeared a little undesirable didn't mean they weren't respectable guests.

"Let's go." Jack tugged on Megan's hand. "Before he changes his mind."

An elevator appeared to be waiting for them. The instant Jack pushed the button, the doors opened. They stepped aboard, and Jack chose the twenty-first floor. When the doors parted on that floor, he turned to the left and strode to the end of the corridor. He hadn't been there for six years, but he would never forget the location of the condo, with its view of the lake in one direction and downtown in the other. Megan would be impressed.

Or not. Her family probably had an entire house on the lake. Yet she had been excited about an apartment where she could catch a glimpse of the sky blue water.

At the door, he knocked softly in deference to the hour. Aunt Julie opened the door, petite and elegant even in yoga pants and a long shirt.

He released Megan and held out his hand. "Thanks for letting us come here."

"You know you're always welcome." She ignored his outstretched hand and enveloped him in a flower-scented hug. "So good to see you. I think you've grown another two inches."

Behind him, Megan snorted.

Ears hot, Jack extricated himself from the embrace and made introductions. They entered the flat, the living room with its panoramic view and plush furniture to one side, a dining room to the other. "Do you want anything to eat or drink? I have tea and cocoa and coffee, though it's late."

"A glass of water and a bed are all I need, thank you." Megan sounded quieter than usual and seemed to droop. Even her curls seemed to have lost their vibrancy.

"You look tired." Aunt Julie cupped Megan's elbow and guided her down the corridor to the room that had always been Grace's. "I think you know where to go," his aunt called over her shoulder.

Jack knew—a pullout bed in his aunt's home office. He didn't even warrant a guest room.

Yet Julie had worked hard to make the place comfortable. The bed was out and made up with pillows and a comforter. An extra toothbrush, razor and towels lay on the bathroom vanity, along with a set of pajamas. And she had stuck a sticky note to her computer monitor with necessary passwords should he need to connect to email or the internet.

He probably did need to, but he doubted he could see the screen for more than a few minutes before his eyes crossed with fatigue. He just wanted to sleep so he could think in the morning. Six hours would be good. Eight would be better.

He readied himself for bed and slipped beneath the comforter, falling asleep almost immediately. He intended to set an alarm, so when his phone rang while the sky over the lake was still dark, he thought at first the alarm was going off.

"Why did I set it so early?" he grumbled as he reached for the phone.

By the time it rested in his palm, he realized he had

gotten the telephone ringtone mixed up with the alarm. An unknown number was calling him.

He was awake in a snap, sitting up, heart racing. "Yes?"

"Mr. Luskie," said an unfamiliar voice, "this is your security company…"

Someone had set off the alarm. They had called the police to investigate and wanted to ensure Jack was all right.

"I'm not there and can't get there for probably an hour." He searched for his clothes, unable to find them anywhere. Instead, a terry robe lay across the bottom of the bed. Aunt Julie's work. She had probably taken his clothes to wash, and he had no idea where the laundry room was.

"I'll get there as fast as I can."

Which wasn't fast at all. Julie slowed him down. His clothes weren't dry yet, so he may as well shower and eat breakfast. Jack wondered when she slept.

He did as she advised. When he emerged from the bathroom, his clothes lay fresh and still warm from the drier over the back of a chair. He dressed and shoved his things into his pockets. He could forgo breakfast.

But when he walked through the dining room to the kitchen, he found his uncle and aunt standing at the counter where the coffee maker gurgled its last drops of fresh brew into the carafe. Dave was just hanging up the landline. He turned to Jack, his face white.

Jack thought he was going to be sick. "My house?" He barely got out the words.

"It's all right, thanks to a sharp-eyed rookie. If it weren't for that…" Dave rubbed his jaw, whiskers rasping beneath his palm. "Jack, that alarm was set off on purpose. Someone wanted you to go home."

"Why?" Jack posed the question, but he had a good idea about the answer, or something close.

"Your house," Dave pronounced, "was wired for a bomb to go off the instant you opened one of the doors."

ELEVEN

"Will you think I'm a horrible person if I tell you I'm glad you're in the hospital?" Megan perched on the edge of a chair beside her boss's bed. "I mean, I'm sorry you're still on oxygen, but I don't know where else—" Her voice broke. She cleared her throat and tried again. "But I don't know where else I can talk to you and not worry...much."

She doubted anyone would try to blow up a hospital just to kill her and Jack. Jack's house and her own apartment were out of the question at the moment. Bomb squads had been sent to both, Jack's house to disarm what was there, and her apartment to ensure nothing was there.

Feeling followed, or that the Cahill connection was looking up everyone she knew with the skill of an experienced PI, Megan didn't want to bring anyone else into this. They might end up the next target.

She felt as though she had a giant bull's-eye painted on her back. On the way to the hospital, she had considered stopping at a pharmacy and buying hair color. Or at a salon to cut off the long curls for something more manageable. Anything to disguise herself.

She also wanted to go to the beach path and run as fast and as far as she could to lessen the tension of adrenaline racing through her veins. And, for the first time in seven years, she wanted to call her family and warn them to be careful.

Of course she would do no such thing. They would use that as an excuse to remind her she had chosen a dangerous profession and they would still support her through law school or medical school or even an MBA. She would have to repeat that she hated all those options, that being a PI was rarely dangerous, and she liked what she was doing.

Most of the time.

She didn't like sitting at her boss's hospital bedside because he was still there after showing signs of pneumonia. Given his age, the doctors had chosen precautions and kept him there with an oxygen cannula hooked on his nose and a disgruntled expression on his face.

"I never would have assigned this case to you if I thought it would have gone sideways like this." Gary's voice still rasped from the smoke damage to his throat. "Workmen's comp fraud is usually pretty cut-and-dried."

"I know. I've done at least half a dozen before." Megan fixed Gary with a glare. "But to whom else would you have assigned the case if you knew it would end up dangerous?"

Gary let out a wheezing laugh. "You and your boarding school grammar. To *whom*. Who talks like that outside the Northwestern English department?"

Megan stiffened. "I do, and I've never been near the Northwestern English department."

The university was far too close to home for her liking.

"And you're avoiding answering my question," Megan added.

"I know." Gary sighed, coughed. "You're the best I have, though Mel might be tougher."

Megan's scowl grew.

Gary grinned. "Can't resist teasing you, Meg."

"Were you teasing me when you sent Jack Luskie to—what do you call it?—keep an eye on me during my investigation?"

"He told you, did he?" Gary kneaded his forehead as though trying to manipulate an answer to emerge. "I got worried when I found out Cahill was being investigated for embezzlement. Malingering so you can get more money from workmen's comp is one thing. Embezzling a few hundred thousand dollars is quite another."

"You couldn't have just told me she might be… touchy?" Megan blinked back a sudden rush of moisture in her eyes.

She would not let Gary know she could get so angry she cried. She wouldn't let him know his lack of faith in her was the cause of that tear-producing anger.

"You couldn't just pull me from the job. You had to send a babysitter?"

"I'm getting too old to have gone with you myself. The ticker isn't so good anymore." He thumped his chest. "But I didn't want you to lose the job, either. I know the commission is important to you, and I couldn't be of much help if trouble came."

"Which it did," Megan said.

"And you didn't have an old man to slow you down."

She didn't know his age but guessed he was somewhere near seventy. His mind was still sharp. He could take bits and pieces of facts and boil them into answers with the speed of a computer finding the square root of ten thousand. But his body, wounded from twenty years in the military, was starting to give out, at least for the sometimes-physical demands of the job.

"Stop trying to gain my sympathy." Megan had to pretend to be hard-hearted. "I didn't need a babysitter."

"Call me a chauvinist if you like, but I prefer to think of it as chivalry."

Megan snorted. "If you don't think women can do the job, then why do you hire only women?"

"Thinking about changing that. We should have at least one man—"

"You're procrastinating."

Gary grinned, sending the cord of the cannula bobbing on his wrinkled cheek. "All right. Jack called me about our end of the case, and I told him I had my best investigator on it."

"Trying to butter me up?"

"He said he didn't know if it was a good idea for you to be going near there alone at night. He said he was finding some pretty serious theft, and people did irrational things when they had that much time in prison waiting for them if they're caught."

"Apparently." Megan slumped forward, her elbows on her knees. "And now we have murder and attempted murder."

The room fell silent save for the hiss of the oxygen and the usual hospital noises outside the room—patients calling for help, staff calling orders back and forth, the squeak of wheels on a cart. Megan thought she heard Jack's voice in the corridor, then a woman laughing. Janet, Gary's wife. Megan would know that lilting sound of mirth anywhere.

Suddenly, she wanted to run into the hallway and ask for a hug. She meant Janet, yet her mind envisioned Jack's strong arms around her.

She shook her head, sending her ponytail bobbing. "Okay, so it was chivalry."

"And a good thing he was there," Gary added.

"Why, so two of us can be in danger?"

"Better the two of you together than trying to get through life alone." He coughed. "I mean danger alone."

Megan opened her mouth to deny the truth of his words, then shut it again. Her truth was she was glad she wasn't going through this alone. She had gone alone through too much in her life.

"So what do we do now?" Megan asked, because Gary's advice was the best she knew.

"Lie low and let the cops handle things from now on."

"And where do I lie low?"

"Go home."

"But my apartment—"

"I don't mean to Edgewater. I mean go home to North Point, to your family."

Megan shot to her feet, spinning to face him. "No way."

"Because they'll say 'I told you so'?" Gary's dark eyes were sharp on hers.

Megan swallowed, nailed.

"I don't want to endanger them, either." Legitimate as the excuse was, it was still an excuse for not going to her family. For not facing her family.

"Do you really think even the wildest of murderers would go after the family of the mayor of North Point?" Gary asked.

"Why not? They've targeted families of federal judges."

Gary's gaze didn't waver.

Megan broke eye contact first. She glanced toward the window, found the view uninspiring, void of answers or more excuses.

"I'll think about it," she conceded.

* * *

What if Grace had gone home with him?

The question haunted Jack as he waited for Megan to finish talking to Gary. As he talked to Gary's wife. As he paced the hospital waiting room.

Grace usually walked in first. He let her so she could sit as soon as possible. She would have been killed. He probably would have been, as well. Still... Grace had done nothing to deserve her life being put into peril.

Neither had Jack, other than worry about the safety of a woman he had never met and witness what she had—violence. He knew too much about Cahill's greed. He had found the path her embezzlement had taken. As he hadn't yet reported all his findings to her employer, the people who had hired him, he might have endangered his life that way. Though surely the Cahill connection wouldn't have known about him. They shouldn't have known about him.

Except Cahill was, apparently, an excellent computer hacker. She might have gotten information on him from her employer's system, if they had been foolish enough to write emails about his being hired.

They shouldn't have. They should have kept it all offline. People didn't think that way, though. They put everything where others could reach it. That made his job easier in the long run. One could always find an electronic trail with patience.

Jack considered himself a patient person. Or had. Not now. Now he was a man needing a long walk or even run in the fresh air.

That true deep autumn had descended on the Midwest meant the weather was a little too fresh for most people, yet Jack considered the cold air might blow the cobwebs from his brain and help him think what to do next. What he and Megan should do next. They were in this together.

Together. Such an odd thought. He was never together with anyone. He didn't have time. Now he was moving away and didn't have the inclination. Megan and he had, however, been thrown together. He wouldn't abandon her until this Cahill connection was behind bars and they were both safe.

He reached the end of the too small—for pacing, anyway—waiting room and turned back just as Megan appeared in the doorway. She stood with her arms crossed over her front. The green of her eyes seemed duller, shadowed with more than fatigue, and her lips quivered as though she wanted to open her mouth and howl in frustration or fear.

"Let's go for a run," Jack said.

Though they still trembled, Megan's lips curved into a smile. "Best idea I've heard all day."

By silent consent, they left the hospital and made their way to the lake path. The waves were high beneath an east wind, rising up with white caps along their tops and sending spray that sometimes reached anyone on the path.

"Can we pace ourselves?" Megan asked. "I'm not sure I can keep up with you."

His legs were a great deal longer than hers, so he kept his stride short, matching his gait to hers. He would have liked to go faster, run as hard and as long as he could, but he wouldn't leave her behind.

One mile passed. Two. Three. His face, hair and one sleeve were soaked with spray. The freshness of air from the lake filled his nose, his lungs. His body seemed to open, renewed, refreshed. As clouds blew in over the water, they seemed to blow out of his head, waking him, rousing his need to succeed, not fail. Not slink away like a coward.

Beside him, Megan picked up her pace. She waved to him, sprinting faster and faster. He lengthened his stride to keep up with her. Blood roared in his ears, as loud as the pounding waves beside them. He felt strong, invigorated. Rejuvenated.

He laughed and slowed to a halt when Megan stopped, bent at the waist, hands on her knees.

"That will probably kill me." She breathed hard. "I haven't run that fast since high school track."

"Were you on the team?" Jack asked.

"Just junior varsity. I'm too short for true speed." She straightened. "What about you?"

"I played baseball."

"I can see that." She nodded, ponytail bouncing.

The shadows had left her eyes, and her lips appeared firm. Soft—

He yanked his gaze away. He didn't need to look at her lips and think that way. They were partners in need for protection, not anything else. And yet…

He turned to stare at the water, dark gray with the approaching storm. "Did your talk with Gary go all right?"

"That depends on your definition of *all right*." She moved to stand beside him, her own gaze fixed on the roiling waves. "He's being overprotective of me. And now he wants me to go ask my family for shelter."

Jack startled. "Why?"

"Because they live in a house too big for any ten people to live in, have a good security system, and my mother is mayor of North Point."

Something roiled like the waves inside Jack. "So I've heard."

"Of a small suburb. She'll be a state senator next." Her nose wrinkled.

"You don't approve?"

"I don't have anything against her political ambitions. I didn't have anything against her career ambitions. But I wanted a mom, too." She wrapped her arms across her middle as though she were cold. "Do you understand?"

"I think so." He pictured his own mom, smiling and warm and always quick with a hug or something to eat, whatever the situation called for. "I had a mom. She didn't work outside the home, but she worked. She ran a home day care. But she was always there." He swallowed and blinked against the lake mist in his eyes. "Until she wasn't."

"I'm sorry you lost her." Megan laid her hand on his arm. "And your dad, too?"

"Three months later. On the job. A domestic violence call gone bad. But I think he didn't much care what happened to him anymore." He covered her hand with his. "Their love for one another was amazing."

"That's wonderful." She blinked hard. Lake mist or tears?

A drop of water rolled down her cheek, and Jack received his answer—tears.

He captured it with the pad of his thumb. "Should I ask what's up, or should I already know?"

She huffed a brief laugh. "You should already know. Or guess. Just me, the spoiled little rich girl, who thinks her parents love one another, but isn't quite sure. Feeling sorry for myself is all."

"I've only known you for two days, but I'd say they did a good job raising you, regardless of the spoiling."

"I think so. They insisted I work hard. I had to take summer jobs, for example. That's how I ended up working for Gary. I was studying criminal justice, and it seemed like a good way to get a different perspective on the law. A month doing research for him, and I was hooked."

"But your family doesn't approve."

She looked down and tugged at her jacket. "They want me behind a desk wearing heels and a suit. Something safe and stable. So you can see why I can't go to them for help right now."

"Do you have another option?" Jack squeezed her fingers, hoping she'd look at him.

She shook her head. "I mean, other than finding a cheap motel and holing up until this person is caught. Or these people. But that's not going to work, either. I can't just shut down my life."

"I understand that. I have to work. I have other clients."

"So do I." She did glance up then. "Is your office all right? Grace said you work from your home."

"It has a garden apartment under the house with a separate entrance, so I use that for an office. The rent is cheap."

"And I have to replace computers for the office and pick out new furniture and rugs and make sure they get installed and make sure everyone can keep working so they can keep getting paid. I think Gary's heart is worse than he's let on, and this hasn't helped." Her shoulders slumped as though all those computers and furnishings rested on her back. "I can't do all that from North Point."

"That makes sense to me."

If she were Grace, he would wrap his arm around her shoulders. But she wasn't his sister. His interest in having his arm around her wasn't in the least sisterly.

He clasped his hands together behind his back. “I understand where you’re coming from.”

“I thought you might.” The shadows had gone from her eyes as she gazed into his. The hollows above her cheekbones still held dark circles of fatigue, but her eyes seemed clearer, brighter, greener than they had earlier.

“Any ideas what to do?” he asked.

“Keep going and try to find out who is doing this.”

“Will you go to your family?”

She shook her head.

“If I can forgive my uncle—”

She held up a “stop” hand. “What happened with your uncle is the past. My parents haven’t forgotten a thing and won’t stop trying to run my life.” She rubbed her upper arms. “We’d better get going. That storm isn’t far off.”

He could see the rain a ways offshore, sheets of silver pounding the waves flat. Hand in hand, they jogged up the beach, back the way they had come, but not as far, for the rain had begun in spits and spatters, and they took refuge in the minuscule entryway of an apartment building with an unlocked outer door. A radiator blasted hot air beneath a row of mailboxes, and they stood before it, their clothes steaming.

Though Jack was warm in an instant, Megan continued to shiver.

“I feel like the cold has gone all the way to my bone marrow.” She spoke between chattering teeth.

“Will this help?” He removed his jacket and wrapped it around her shoulders.

“Thanks.” She pulled it tight. It was twice her size.

Jack fastened the neck snap beneath her chin, then cupped her cheeks in his hands. Her skin was smooth and flawless without a speck of makeup. A natural beauty who wasn't vain about her looks. She presented herself to the world as she was, without pretense.

"You're something special," he told her because he couldn't stop himself.

"I am?" She blinked up at him. "Why would you think that? Because I won't trade what I believe is my calling for lots of money?"

"That, too. But I was thinking because you're honest and kind and brave and…" He sighed, not because he had run out of complimentary adjectives, but because of what he was about to do. Because he knew he shouldn't, and yet, when her lashes fluttered, half concealing her eyes, when her lips parted in a silent gasp, he gave in.

And he kissed her.

TWELVE

Megan couldn't remember the last time she had been kissed. At that moment, she thought maybe she had never been kissed. Certainly no kiss had made her feel like she was soaring along the shoreline. No, above the shoreline. Flying.

Then a car horn blasted in the street, and they jerked apart as though someone had shoved them in opposite directions.

Jack scrubbed his hands over his face. "I guess I shouldn't have done that. I had no right. I—"

"Please don't apologize." Megan's face felt as red as her hair. "I didn't exactly push you away."

The idea of doing so hadn't even occurred to her. She might examine that later, but she already suspected she knew the answer—she had wanted him to kiss her. When they had been standing on the shore, with the wild waves and clouds pushing toward them, when they had been standing on her balcony. When—

"I'm not in a position for a relationship," Jack said.

"Neither am I." She stared at her sandy and wet running shoes, the wet hems of her jeans. "I have an agency to get recovered from this debacle."

"I'm moving to Virginia in March."

"I'm trying to stay alive right now."

"I have a sister who still needs to heal."

They fell silent. Megan avoided looking at him. From the position of his body, she guessed he wasn't glancing her way, either.

Beyond the glass door, rain splashed down onto the sidewalk like a waterfall. Cars plowing through the flooding street added to the tumult, spattering and hissing and soaking passersby. Above them, someone turned on a stereo with a bass that nearly shook the walls.

Megan's head began to pound in rhythm.

"Now we got all that stuff out of the way," she said, "I want to go home. And I don't mean to North Point."

"You can't."

"You and what army are going to stop me?" Megan shot him her fiercest glare.

Jack took another step away from her so his back was to the opposite wall and glared right back. "I can't, but there's still a killer out there who'd like to add you to his tally."

"You, too. Where will you go?"

"My uncle's, I suppose."

"At least alone at my place, I don't need to worry about anyone else getting hurt." She caught her breath, realizing at once how unkind her words could be if taken the wrong way. "I didn't mean you were endangering your sister and aunt. I was purely referring to myself. I know you'd always take Grace into consideration first, and…and…"

That was why she had wanted, welcomed, succumbed to the kiss—Jack was such a kind and good man. His love and tenderness toward his sister were enough to melt the hardest heart, and Megan's was far from hard. At least it was far from hard where everyone except her family was concerned.

Ugh. She shouldn't have a hard heart toward them, either.

Her stomach rolled. "I'm calling a rideshare." She dug her phone from her pocket. "We can drop you at the nearest L station."

"I'll go with you."

Megan's head shot up. "You'll what?"

"Let me come with you so I can make sure your place is safe. I'll leave right after. I'd just feel better if I can see no one unpleasant is around."

"Unpleasant?" That made Megan laugh. "Understatement incarnate." She tapped out her request. "I'll let you go with me and play cop to make sure the boogeyman isn't hiding in a closet or tampering with my gas line."

"Thanks for that image. I just want to die knowing I'm taking everyone else with me."

She clicked the button for requesting the ride. "Five minutes."

Five silent minutes. She didn't know what to say to Jack. His kissing her had taken their relationship from companions in a dangerous situation to—what? Nothing. They couldn't continue to be just friends after showing one another how they had begun to feel about the other. At the same time, those feelings had no future. Even if Jack weren't going away, Megan's job would surely interfere. She still heard her mother saying loud and clearly, *No man will want to marry a woman who is going somewhere any time of the day or night.*

And yet her father had married her mother. She'd been a corporate lawyer who often stayed at the office half the night or longer working on a crucial deadline for a client. Her father was a plastic surgeon and rarely had emergencies. Still he had married Megan's mom. They had three children. And one thing Megan never doubted was that they loved and respected and admired one another even forty years later, after Mother had dropped the law offices for politics, and Father spent more time wielding a golf club than a scalpel.

Regardless of what had worked for her parents, Megan would not compromise between her career and a potential relationship. Or maybe a relationship at all.

The five minutes crept by. The apartment foyer seemed to grow smaller with each second. Jack was so close. Too close. With little movement, she could take his hand in hers, touch his face—

Her phone pinged to notify her that her ride had appeared. She spotted the sedan drawing up the curb, slammed the panic bar on the door and fled across the sidewalk. Jack followed. She sensed rather heard him coming after her. Once inside the vehicle, she slid across the seat as far as she could. Jack swung himself in and closed the door. He was too big. He took up too much of the back seat. They had been in a smaller car the other night, and she hadn't minded that. Only now, only after he had kissed her, did she feel like she needed to build a barricade between them, something strong and wide.

She concentrated on her breathing. Long, slow breaths. Another five minutes to her house. That was all. Another five minutes after that for him to inspect her apartment for signs of an intruder. She could manage that.

Yet once they reached her apartment, she noticed his hair was damp from the rain, heard her own stomach growling, and thought of the long ride home he still had.

"I'm not much of a cook," she said, "but I can manage a sandwich."

"That would be good of you." He didn't look directly at her. "Let's look at things first."

They looked. Doors and windows were locked. None

of the bottles, brushes or other containers on tables and dressers were moved. Not so much as a toothbrush had shifted a centimeter out of the bathroom holder. The only thing moving in the apartment were drifts of the ever-present golden retriever fur. Megan and Amber ran an automatic vacuum, and Amber brushed Tess every day, but still the hair managed to infiltrate every nook and cranny. Megan felt the dog's absence. She could have used something warm to hug.

She would not let her gaze drift to Jack.

She hastened to put together sandwiches. She thought about but did not make coffee. She was on edge enough without more caffeine in her system. And coffee encouraged lingering. She didn't want to linger across a table from Jack.

Didn't want was the wrong sentiment. She *dared not want*.

They chatted about inconsequential things as they ate. The weather was a safe topic.

"Pretty cold for the middle of October," Megan said.

"Could end up a rough winter."

Snow and the polar vortex of winters past took up half a sandwich each. The World Series took up the next half. Megan could talk baseball through a three-course meal—and had. She spent much time listening to games on the radio while on a stakeout.

A stakeout. Her car.

She sighed. "I want my car back."

"Won't your insurance pay for a rental?" Jack asked.

"They will, but I have so much paperwork to do for that to happen, then getting the car and all. I just haven't had time."

"Maybe you can do some of it online today." Jack

glanced around the kitchen. "Are you sure you're comfortable alone here?"

"As comfortable as I can be anywhere." She stood, removing their empty plates from the table. "Face it—breaking in here is pretty hard. I'm on the third floor beyond a locked door, then another locked door. A thousand people live within a hundred feet. Someone would hear me scream. And no one else will get hurt here on my account."

At least she hoped the tenants of the other two apartments in the building wouldn't come to harm because of her. They shouldn't unless the Cahill connection decided to bomb the building or burn it down. Fire was always a concern. The building was over 100 years old and mostly wood.

Her stomach knotted around the smoked turkey she had just consumed. "Right now, I want a good book and a good nap."

Jack smiled. "Hint taken." He slipped on his jacket and headed for the door. "Lock up behind me and don't open the door to strangers."

She rolled her eyes.

Jack left without another word or backward glance.

Megan locked the door—all three locks—the handle lock, a dead bolt with a keyhole on the outside, and a dead bolt without a keyhole outside. Then she changed into dry sweats, put some soft music on her iPad and curled up on the sofa with the sort of detective novel that made her cringe yet still enjoy.

She was half-asleep when she heard the yowl. The rain had stopped, the traffic diminished, or she wouldn't have been able to hear anything on the ground. But it had grown quiet enough the yowling sounded like an ambulance siren. An animal was frightened or hurt.

Megan sprang to her feet, letting her book thud to the floor, and sprinted for the balcony doors. She doubted she would see anything from her floor but she might get the attention of a passerby to check out the cat calling for help—or maybe just expressing her displeasure with life and the state of the world.

She flipped the locks on the doors and crossed the planks to lean over the railing.

And the railing bowed beneath her weight. The crack of splintering wood ricocheted off the building like a gunshot. Megan sprawled as though she'd been shot. She gripped the spindles, felt the tilt. The downward tilt. She kicked, trying to find the balcony floor with her feet. No good. Each movement sent the rail pointing more and more toward the ground. The more the railing bent, the more Megan slid. The more she slid, the worse grew the slant in the wrong direction. In moments, her feet would dangle above the sidewalk forty feet below.

If the railing didn't break free first.

Jack heard Megan's scream from the alley where he had gone to look for the crying cat. Unable to leave Megan alone in her apartment, he had chosen to remain on her street, patrolling, circling, watching her building for anything suspicious. He wanted to keep her safe.

And he had failed. Someone had gotten to her, and she was in danger…or worse.

He raced around the building, dialing 911 as his feet pounded the pavement. He glanced toward her apartment and found her faster than he thought he could. Faster than he wanted to. She hung above him like some new gymnastics trick of swinging through parallel bars forty feet above the ground.

"Hang on," he shouted.

"Thanks. I thought I'd let go."

Somehow her good Midwest sarcasm comforted him. She still possessed her sense of humor.

"I called 911." He positioned himself beneath her.

He could probably catch her if she fell. She was pretty small. He could bear her weight. They both might fall to the sidewalk, but at least she would not be a smashed heap of broken bones.

But if the railing crashed down, as well, they were in trouble. Ten or twelve feet long and four feet high, it must weigh hundreds of pounds. Hundreds of pounds of solid wood, not wimpy plywood.

And if it wasn't made of flimsy boards, how had it come loose?

Later. Later he would examine how the railing had been tampered with. He considered no ifs in this situation. Someone had sabotaged that railing figuring Megan would lean against it at some point. Megan or one of her friends.

Jack's insides felt as though someone were using them for shoelaces. Pulled taut. Knotted.

"I'll catch you if you fall," he called to Megan.

"And end up a human pancake on the sidewalk?" Her vibrant curls bobbed. "I think—"

Above, the railing groaned.

"Stand back," someone yelled.

Jack glanced around to find a crowd forming on the sidewalk. Cars had stopped in the middle of the street, drivers and passengers emerging to watch the show.

"Clear the street," Jack called to the stopped vehicles. "Emergency vehicles can't get through."

The drivers ignored him.

"That railing's going to go." An old man dressed in a flannel shirt and overalls, as though he'd just left his downstate farm, plucked at Jack's arm. "You'd better move back, son."

"I need to stay here so I can catch her."

He wanted the old man to leave. He might be able to catch Megan and run if the railing began to break away from the balcony. The elderly gentleman would never survive.

"I'll be fine," Jack said.

"I don't think so." The man's grip on Jack's arm tightened. "Get yourself out of the way."

"Speaking of getting out of the way." Jack tried to be casual, while his heart pounded hard enough to shake a stadium. "Someone with authority needs to get those cars moving out of the street."

The wail of a siren rang across the city.

"Do you think you can talk the drivers into moving along?"

Or the rest of the crowd.

He'd done some crowd control once. Day after Thanksgiving sales with stressed and excited shoppers pushing and shoving one another away from the store doors. This wasn't the same. These people were quiet, faces filled with the horror Jack felt. A woman was about to plunge to her death, and they wanted to be witnesses before the evening news.

And here came the media. A photographer talking into a mic arrived before the firetruck. Filming, filming, filming what might be Megan's last moments.

The killer's victory moments.

An ominous crack reverberated from above. The railing had broken away from one end and begun to swing both down and to the side.

Megan screamed.

The emergency personnel were still too far away. Only a block, but that was too far.

Jack positioned himself beneath Megan and held up his arms. “Let go.”

“I can’t. My fingers… Stuck.”

Cramped from holding on so hard.

“Just try one at a time,” Jack encouraged her. “You can do it. We can do it.”

Megan said something, but the cameraman interrupted. “Do you know her, sir?”

“Yes.” Jack didn’t look at him. He kept his focus on Megan. “Come on, sweetheart. First finger, go. Second.”

“I—” The railing broke away at the next spindle, and Megan’s cry must have been heard all the way to Indiana.

The rumble of the firetruck blocked her words this time. Men in heavy geared leaped out and grabbed for a ladder. That would work.

If they got it in place soon enough.

They wouldn’t be soon enough. Already Megan’s hands were giving way. Cramped or not, fingers could only hold a person’s weight for so long. That long had passed for her. With a shriek from Megan and a gasp from the crowd, she began to fall.

THIRTEEN

Jack sprang. Megan struck him as though the entire balcony had fallen. His arms closed around her. Together they crashed to the ground, Jack twisting to ensure he landed on the bottom, cushioning her fall. Wind left his lungs in a whoosh.

Around them, cheers and applause broke out. Cameras flashed.

“Just what I want,” Megan murmured in Jack’s ear. “Another fifteen minutes of fame.”

Though he lay on his back on concrete, still unable to wholly catch his breath, Jack felt as though he soared. Megan was a remarkable woman. So resilient. So strong. He felt privileged to know her even for these few days.

“I crushed you.” She started to rise.

“Don’t move, miss.” A paramedic hustled forward. “You might have broken something. We need to put you on a backboard and have you x-rayed.”

“I’m not the one who probably broke something.” She shifted onto the pavement and sat up. “It’s him.”

“All right.” Jack managed to get the two words out on wheezing breaths. “Just wind knocked out.”

“Amazing catch, sir.” The cameraman crowded in. “Will you tell us what you know about what happened?”

"You saw most of what I saw." Jack pushed himself to a sitting position.

"Sir," the paramedic protested.

"Whose apartment is that?" a fireman asked.

"Mine." Megan raised one hand, revealing a palm full of splinters.

"I can tend to those." Happy to have something he could do, the paramedic guided Megan off to the ambulance to have the splinters removed and disinfected.

"We need to inspect that railing," the fireman said. "Do you know how we can get up there?"

"I doubt she had her keys with her. Maybe the landlord."

The emergency over, the crowd began to disburse, but one tenant came forward. "The landlord's on his way. I called him as soon as I saw what was happening." He shook his head and hunched his shoulders to his ears as though trying to draw into a protective shell. "I lean on my balcony railing all the time."

"So does Megan." Jack didn't know that for sure. He couldn't. He didn't know enough about her to know those little details of her life, yet he saw so clearly her leaning on that railing, talking about her glimpse of the lake, and he was sure he was right.

"Thanks for your help," Jack said.

Ignoring questions from the original cameraman and other reporters who had shown up, Jack made his way to the ambulance. Megan sat on the bumper, one paramedic holding her hand, palm up, the other using fine tweezers to pull out splinters and dab ointment on the wounds, along with tending to several scrapes on her palms and wrists. Her face was white, and Jack didn't think the tremble of her lips had anything to do with him.

"Thank you," she said. "You saved my life."

"Someone would have caught you."

She shook her head. "I don't think so. You were the only one close enough."

"I think there were…" Jack began.

Then an old song, one recorded before he was born, ran through his head. Something about only having eyes for one person. If she only had eyes for him, they were in trouble. They were caring too much for one another for two people without a future together.

As he had known when he kissed her.

His knees wobbled. He wished he had somewhere to sit.

He settled for crouching on the sidewalk in front of Megan. "Can you tell me what happened yet, or do you need a break first?"

"I can tell you." She swallowed. "The cops are going to want a report anyway. Ugh." She pressed her forearm over her eyes. "Another police report."

"Either you're a wanted woman or accident-prone," one paramedic joked.

"I am a wanted woman, but not like you mean. Someone wants to kill me."

The paramedics stared at her.

"She's not paranoid," Jack said. "It's the truth. So don't think she has something wrong with her when she tells you she thinks that balcony railing was tampered with."

"I think it was," Megan said. "That railing has been as solid as—as something solid since I've lived here. It didn't just go bad in a day."

"And you were leaning on it yesterday, and I checked it to see how sturdy it was," Jack added.

The mouths of the paramedics were sagging open. But they didn't have time for questions. A police detective strolled up and began firing questions at Megan like bullets at a range. Halfway through the questioning, he received a phone call. He walked away and turned his back on them. When he returned, he fixed them with cold, nearly black eyes. "I understand you two are in the middle of a murder investigation."

"We're not suspects," Megan said.

"This isn't the first attempt on our lives," Jack added.

The detective handed each of them his card. "I need a full report. Come to the station at your earliest convenience."

"One more trip to a police station is never convenient," Megan grumbled.

Jack grinned at her and squeezed her shoulder. "You should be an expert at making reports by now."

"Apparently useless ones." Suddenly, she jerked away from him and held his gaze with two green spears. "How did you get here so fast anyway?"

"I, um, never left." Jack broke their gazes. "I didn't want you here alone."

"Because I need a protector." Her lips quivered in a way that shook Jack's resolve to not get involved.

Not too involved.

"Looks like you're fortunate he decided to stick around," one of the paramedics put in. "Not sure anyone else would have been here quick enough to catch you."

"Or been strong enough," the other added. He rubbed his slim arms. "You fell before the firemen could decide how to get you down."

This time when Megan looked into his eyes, hers had softened from pointed emeralds to soft spring grass. "I haven't thanked you. If the fall hadn't killed me, it would have seriously injured me."

"Seriously." Jack's voice sounded like he spoke over gravel even to himself.

"Both legs broken at least," the older and brawnier of the two paramedics said.

Megan emitted a shaky laugh. "Thanks for that vision. I mean, no thanks."

"Happy to oblige." The paramedic held out his hands to help her rise. "You should go to a doctor to have your hands checked out. Especially if you get any swelling."

"You might have broken a couple of metacarpal bones," the other medic said.

Megan paled.

Jack shot a glare at the two emergency workers. "I think that's enough."

"Tetanus shot," the older medic said. "When did you last have one?"

"A year ago." Megan glanced from her bandaged hands to Jack. "And what about the cat? Did you hear the cat?"

"I did." Jack nodded toward the alley. "I heard one yowling back there and went to see if I could find him. Otherwise, I would have been here when the railing broke."

"Like Romeo calling under my balcony?" Megan clamped her hand over her mouth as though wishing she could push the words back.

Jack experienced a need to go for another run on the beach path.

"Let's hope our ending is better than theirs."

It would be because they wouldn't have entered into a doomed relationship.

"Do you want to go back upstairs?" Jack asked her.

"No. I want to look for the cat. It was crying so badly I was sure it was injured." She blinked hard. "I think someone made it meow so I'd go onto the balcony. And if they hurt an animal to get to me..." She flashed a fierce scowl in Jack's direction as though he was responsible for a possibly injured cat. “They’ll be sorry.” She sighed. “That was kind of weak, wasn’t it?”

“I hope I never make you angry.” Jack touched her elbow, wanting only to make her happy. “Let’s go look for Mittens.”

Megan rolled her eyes in Jack’s direction. “You couldn’t come up with anything better than Mittens?”

“Muffin?”

“Worse.”

“Xena?”

“Let’s find her first.” Instead of thinking about the unnamed cat, Jack found himself thanking God for Megan still being alive, for Megan being alive at all and coming into his life.

Megan headed in the direction opposite from where the balcony had come down. She couldn’t so much as get a glimpse of that pile of splintered wood she’d once thought sturdy, unbreakable.

She’d once thought herself unbreakable. Simple, stakeout jobs bored her. She wanted chases and excitement.

She still did, but not with the same ferocity as before. Being chased wasn’t as much fun as she had imagined it would be. A few weeks or even months sitting behind a computer researching databases sounded like the most exciting work she wanted for a while.

She would do that. She would have her agency. But not until they caught the person or persons behind the Cahill murder.

So now she was heading into an alley to look for a cat, as though a cat could give her answers or clues. Or maybe she could rescue it and feel as though she were accomplishing something.

The alley was empty. No people. No cat.

Megan's limbs felt limp, heavy like waterlogged newspapers. She turned back to her building, thinking of the forty-two steps she had to climb.

"I need to pack some things," she said. "I need to figure out where to go."

She didn't move. She leaned against the corner of the building, brick rough and smelling earthy against her cheek. Visions of her parents' home raced through her head. Solid brick a quarter mile past a gate, perched on a little bluff above the lake. She should go. She should swallow her anger with them—no, she should abandon her anger with them—and beg them for a place to live. Listen to their smug acknowledgement of their superior knowledge of what was good for her. Neither of her brothers, neither of her parents, had ever experienced a life-threatening situation.

She shouldn't have, either. She had simply wanted to close that case so quickly she wouldn't bide her time for Cahill to give herself away.

She reached for her phone and discovered it was no longer in her pocket.

"My phone is gone." She couldn't even exclaim with any enthusiasm.

Jack strode over to lean one hand against the wall. "It probably fell out when you fell. Let's look."

They rounded to the street side again and found what was left of her phone—a leather case with broken shards of plastic, glass and electronic components.

"One more thing to take care of." Megan gathered the pieces Jack handed to her. She would take them to an electronics recycling location when she could. "I guess it's a priority."

She couldn't go without a phone. Sadly, she barely remembered phone numbers anymore and wouldn't be able to contact anyone other than Amber and maybe a couple more people, without those stored on the cloud.

"I'll go with you." Jack looked at the front door. "How do we get in?"

"The landlord's here to let the cops in. I can call—" She let out a little laugh. "We can ring the bell for my apartment."

The landlord responded to her call up to her apartment. In a moment, he had released the lock on the front door and Megan was climbing the steps, Jack behind her, close, as though he believed she would fall backward.

She might. From being able to run up those steps on a good day, she now crept along one at a time, then sat on the first landing to catch her breath and climb the next set.

"You should have gone to the hospital to get checked out," Jack said.

"I hate hospitals."

"Who doesn't? They still have their uses."

"I'm fine." Megan leaned on the bannister. "Or I will be."

She managed the last twenty steps and entered her apartment. It seemed full of people, chaotic. Invaded. She waved Jack to have a seat wherever he could find one and closed herself into her bedroom. A duffel, a few clothes and other personal items, and she was ready to go.

She was just shoving a few books into the outside pockets when Jack called to her and knocked on the door.

"It's Amber," he said.

Megan took the phone. "What's up? You aren't—nothing bad's happened, has it?"

"We're all fine." Amber's shaky voice didn't match her words. "But my mom…" She took a deep breath. "My mom broke her hip, and I have to go home to take care of her for a while."

"Oh no." Megan reached for something solid to hold onto and found Jack's hand, fingers curling around hers, warm and a little calloused. "When… How…"

"Mel's bringing me home to pack more things, and I have a flight out tonight."

"About the apartment," Megan began.

"I know. Megan, I'm so sorry. You should be in the hospital or something. You can't be all right."

"I am. Really."

Except for feeling like she was dangling above that pavement again. Amber leaving felt like abandonment. Like she was being forced to go to the place she had called home for twenty years.

"Where will you go?" Amber asked.

"I don't know." Megan sighed. "To North Point, probably."

She wished they wouldn't be at home.

"Then don't wait for me. I'll be fine with Mel with me."

"And half a dozen cops making a mess of things looking for clues." Megan swallowed a lump in her throat. "Take care of yourself and keep in touch."

"You know I will. I'll be bored to death in that suburb of Mom's without any public transit."

They said their goodbyes, then Amber was gone, and Megan felt hollow.

"I need to find the nearest cell phone store." She reached for her duffel.

Jack picked it up before she could. "Let me help you, Megan." Jack's voice was soft, his gaze intense. "You can't do all this on your own."

"I already dragged you into danger."

Gazing into his eyes, she knew she couldn't stay around him, or she just might want to kiss him again. She wanted to kiss him again at that moment. Stupid.

Reckless. Playing with hearts without a purpose other than comfort that wasn't the sort of comfort she needed.

She tore her gaze away and grabbed her handbag. "I'm ready to go."

But they were stopped by a cop wanting a statement and another telling her the railing had definitely been tampered with. Bolts anchoring the railing to the floor of the balcony had been cut partly through. The balcony was off limits. They would take bolts and other pieces of the railing retrieved from the sidewalk into the crime lab for investigation. Some fingerprints, but probably hers and Amber's. By the time he finished with his explanations, Megan felt numbed by fatigue and shock.

Maybe she should have gone to the hospital. She felt as though she walked through vanilla custard. Every step was an effort, every word harder to process. Without Jack's help, she doubted she could have gotten into a rideshare vehicle and arrived at a cell phone store.

That process seemed to take hours. Fortunately, she had insurance on her phone, so she only had to pay a relatively small fee to replace it. But she needed to download everything from the cloud in order to have phone numbers. Phone numbers and pictures. That infamous video of Cahill. Megan fell asleep waiting for her phone to receive all its new data. Jack woke her when the transfer was done and a dozen texts and missed call signals pinged across her screen. "Do you want to go to your parents' now?" he asked.

"No, but I don't see any choice at this point in time." She looked at her messages. Most were from Amber. Two were from Janet.

And Megan's mother had left one, too.

FOURTEEN

Megan stared at her phone, at the voice mail message indication. Her mother had called her. Her mother had left a message.

This wasn't the first time her mother had called in the past seven years. She never failed to remember Megan's birthday. She invited her to dinner on the major holidays such as Christmas and Thanksgiving. She wanted Megan at the celebration when she'd been elected mayor of North Point. Other than that, they communicated through the attorney who controlled Megan's college fund, then the trust fund. Megan's refusal to continue her education as her parents felt fit had driven a wedge between them that prevented exchanges beyond the formalities. Other than wanting Megan around for a show of family unity, her parents didn't seem to mind the separation any more than Megan did.

Until now. Now her mother's name glowed on the screen like a lighthouse beacon—bright, clear, penetrating the darkness between them.

"What is it?" Jack asked. "Unless it's none of my business, of course."

It kind of wasn't his business. If she told him, he would tell her she had to forgive and should contact her family. That she fully intended to do so wouldn't matter. He would want her to return the call that minute.

But the first contact, the first cry for help she would be giving them in three quarters of a decade should not be through the impersonal means of a wireless phone. She would go to their gate, their door, and she would ask them in person if they would give her shelter.

She swiped the screen clear. "It was my mother."

Jack's eyebrows shot up. "She has your number?"

"Yes, of course. I don't want them to tell me what to do with my life when it's nothing that I want. That doesn't mean I'm a monster. My mother asked for it, so I gave it to her. Other than that, she's respecting my boundaries."

"That's odd."

"How's that?" Megan glanced at him.

"Odd she would call now. You know, just when you need her help."

"She more likely wants to make sure I won't embarrass her somehow." Megan stuffed her phone into her pocket.

"If you're going to ask your mother for help," Jack said, "I think you should listen to her message."

Megan suppressed a momentary irritation. "I will." She spoke with more of a snap than she intended.

Jack merely shrugged off her ill-humor. "Does she watch the twenty-four-hour news cycles?" Jack asked in an offhand manner, his gaze going past Megan's shoulder.

Megan swung around to follow his line of sight to the television mounted on the store wall. The sound was turned down, inaudible, but the picture was loud and clear. There, nearly as large as life on the wide screen, Megan hung from the broken balcony balustrade.

With a groan, Megan ducked her face into her hands. "Of course I'm on the news. That was a spectacular show for everyone else."

"Including the killer," Jack murmured as though he were talking to himself.

He never took his focus from the screen, from the crowd shown around the balcony. His lips moved, but he didn't speak loudly enough for Megan to hear any words. She just read his expression through her fingers and wanted to remain hidden.

He was furious. His blue eyes glowed like lightning. Spots of red burned along his cheekbones. And his lips were thin and tight.

She wanted to soothe him, calm him, assure him this would do no more harm than had already been done. The news feed wouldn't tell the killer or anyone else where they were. Where she was.

She raised her head to look at him directly. "It's done. I can't change it. I couldn't change it while everyone was taking pictures. It's probably all over social media sites."

"Look at the crowd," Jack said. "No, wait." He held up his own phone and began to search. "Look for some of those clips. We might see Cahill's friend in the crowd."

Ignoring dirty looks from the customer service people behind the counter for taking up seats intended for new costumers, none of whom were present in the store, they divided up the social media sites and began to scroll, finding different versions of the video, different angles of the crowd. After a few minutes, everyone appeared the same. Faceless. Nameless. Harmless.

But someone out there was far from harmless.

Megan swiped and squinted and swiped again. She paused streaming content and expanded the size of images. She saw no one familiar after several minutes of scrutinizing at least two dozen videos of herself dangling above the sidewalk. The pictures made her queasy.

That wasn't a stranger. That was her looking terrified and helpless.

The helplessness angered her, and she scrolled faster, swiped with more vigor.

And nearly missed the heavy-browed man at the far edge of her building.

Only half of him showed. The corner of her triplex shielded the rest of him. She had, however, looked at the video of him on Cahill's deck enough to recognize that half a face.

"We can't continue like this." She rose and strode to the door. "We're just running, not catching, and I'm tired of being a fugitive."

Sure she would start jumping up and down and screeching if she didn't move, Megan opened the door to a rush of chilly air. It refreshed her, revived her, cleared the cobwebs from her brain. The man was out there. He was around every time something bad happened, waiting for the consequences. She felt like being foolish and making a target of herself so the man could be captured.

She stepped onto the sidewalk.

"Megan, wait." Jack strode after her, still looking at his phone. "Look at the woman beside him."

Megan paused to study the face of the woman beside the heavy-browed man. She was tall, slender, blonde. She appeared to be Cahill, but not quite. Her eyes were slightly closer together, her lips wider. Other than those slight differences, they could have been the same person. A sister? A cousin?

"At least we know we weren't seeing things that first night." She gave Jack his phone. "I'm sure she's the one with the gun we saw when we were on the bus."

"Me, too. That confirms it. Elizabeth Cahill is the woman I saw dead in her house."

"She stole money for these people, and they killed her." Sadness clutched Megan's spirit. "Why would someone ruin one's life like that? She had a good life, a nice house in a good neighborhood, a good job, no debt other than her mortgage. Millions would sell their souls for less than what she had."

"Millions have sold their souls for less. And millions will continue to do so."

"My soul's worth more than that." Megan brushed her hand across her eyes. "I suppose I should head to my parents' house." She pulled her phone out once more and let it scan her face so she could get to her voicemail. For some reason, her heart began to thump hard and fast, restricting her breathing, the edge of a panic attack at the mere anticipation of hearing her mother speak.

"I can see you are all right," the message began without preamble. "I can also see that job is far more dangerous than you told us it would be. But I need to tell you that you can't come here for shelter."

Megan gasped and pressed her hand to her middle. She was going to be sick. Her last place, her best place, of refuge had just been swept from beneath her feet.

"She can't mean it," Megan whispered, jabbing her thumb against her phone screen until the voicemail message disappeared.

"Mean what?" Jack rested his hand on her shoulder, a warm, solid comfort. "What's wrong?"

"She won't let me go to her house." Megan's eyes watered, burned. "The safest place I know, and she won't let me go there for shelter."

"Is she afraid?"

"Probably. But I'm her daughter." Megan swiped at her eyes as though that would erase the tears as easily as a swipe of her finger erased messages on her phone.

Jack's lips parted as if he were about to speak, then closed them. He glanced away, then back, expression determined. "She needs to think of her safety."

"Right. She's a mayor of a community of rich people. But what about me?"

"Did she offer her help in any way, or was that all she said?"

"She… I…" Her cheeks heated. "I was so angry I deleted the message."

Jack's eyebrows shot up. "Isn't that kind of…of…"

"Childish? Yes." Megan blinked hard. "I seemed to get that way around her."

"I was going to say irresponsible," Jack said.

"Same difference." Megan heaved a sigh. "I still have to go and ask for help."

"Can she keep you out, if her home is so secure?"

"She can, but I'm counting on her not being able to if I show up at her gate."

"What about going to her office instead. Townhall in North Point?"

"Not at all secure. They only scan people for guns who are going into the courthouse side. Besides, it closes at five o'clock."

"How will you get there?"

"I'll catch a commuter train at Ogilvie Station and take a taxi or rideshare from the other end."

"Then let's go." Jack hefted her duffel over his shoulder.

"What do you mean by *let's*?"

"I mean let us be on our way."

"But you can't go to North Point." Megan reached out her hand for her bag. "It's out of your way."

"I can't let you go…alone." The intensity of his blue eyes, the way they bored into hers made Megan suspect that the hesitation between *go* and *alone* held significance. She couldn't help but think he intended to simply say he couldn't let her go.

But of course he could. He would. He was leaving the state in March.

And suddenly she knew she didn't want that to happen.

Wanting it not to happen couldn't stop it, though. She had no right to stop him from fulfilling his dream.

She knew she should have kicked him out of her car on that nighttime street what felt like a lifetime ago.

"I can't go back to my house yet," Jack pointed out. "So the only place I have to go is my aunt and uncle's."

So true, and she would like his companionship. A wingman was better than no man, than being alone.

"Then we should get a move-on." She began to trot to the nearest L station that would take them downtown. The Metra trains left from a station west of the Loop, and they had several blocks to walk once they reached the center of the city.

Oddly, Megan felt safe on the L train. A heater blasted beneath her seat, warming her feet, and Jack sat beside her, his hand over hers where it rested on her handbag, warming her fingers. They said little. They couldn't talk in a crowded train car. She stared at the passing city below, then the people around them. None appeared familiar. None were the heavy-browed man and his blonde accomplice. Of course, they could have disguised themselves and followed. They could have more accomplices Megan and Jack didn't know and thus couldn't recognize. The extraordinarily thin woman on Jack's right could be working with the killers, reporting to them. So could the freckled teen across the aisle.

"They could have moved on when they failed with me," Megan said with more hope than assurance.

"They could have. I doubt they know where we are right now anyway." He tightened his hand on hers.

Warmth tingled up her arm. She wished she could rest her head on his shoulder and dream of no killers after them, of hot chocolate beside a warm fire, even a fake gas fire, of friends laughing and talking. She loved those things about cold autumn nights, or watching the snow fall in the winter.

"I like cold weather," she announced.

Jack chuckled. "A true Midwesterner. I'm glad Virginia gets cold. People say the northern part is pretty moderate."

Of course. Virginia. He was moving to Virginia.

Megan's half daydream faded, and she pulled her hand free. Her fingers were instantly cold. No future. Once they had settled this mess, she doubted she would ever see him again.

"I think Washington, DC, is beautiful in the spring." She looked at the location board and rose, her arm curved around her handbag. Carrying her duffel, Jack followed her off the train and down the steps to street level.

A crowd surrounded them on their way to the commuter train station that carried thousands of people into the suburbs. Safety in crowds. Safety in lighted streets. Safety at the end of the line and her parents' gated community. She would accept their "I told you so" attitude in exchange for safety. She was tired of running. Without anything toward which to run, she would rather find security.

"What about you, Jack?" she asked. "Will you be all right staying with your uncle?"

"Probably better than you staying with your parents, from what you've said."

"You'll have your sister."

"I will. And you'll have your siblings?"

Megan shook her head. "They don't live here. One is in New York, the other in Boston. They're married and have families."

A pang shot through her at how she was missing her nieces and nephews growing up. Somehow, she must change that. Surely God would want her to change it, to make her family a family again.

If only her parents understood being a PI was her calling, as much as her siblings' careers were their calling, their work.

They walked fast, and the half mile to the station sped past. Most people used electronic tickets, so the line before the window was short. Megan bought two tickets to the North Point stop, which was nothing more than a parking lot, and they made their way to the correct departure gate. The train wasn't there yet, so Megan took out her phone and began to scan the settings to see if one could recover voicemail as one could recover deleted email. Deleted text messages were unrecoverable, so she presumed voicemails couldn't be gotten back either. Yet there it was—a section she had never noticed before in an archive of deleted voicemails.

"I can undelete it," Megan said, tapping her screen. "My mother's message."

Surely that would make up for her being so immature as to erase it without hearing her mother through. Too often she shut out her mother's words before she was finished speaking. A bad habit. She would never tolerate it in herself in her PI work. She should never tolerate it in her personal life.

Her mother's voice came through loud and clear once more, playing in speaker mode so Jack could hear. First the part she'd listened to about not being welcome at their house, then the part she had erased in anger and hurt.

"We have relocated ourselves and no one will be at the house. I won't say where we're going. It's best you don't know while people connected with you seem to be in danger."

Megan's hand tightened on her phone so hard Jack feared she would crush it. Her knuckles whitened as pale as her face, but her clenched teeth suggested she suffered more from anger than fear.

"Megan." Jack used his most soothing tone. "She didn't reject you."

"Of course she did." Her face crumpled. "At least that's how it feels."

Megan was such a tough lady, had put up with so much in the past few days without breaking down more than a little. She had kept moving forward knowing she was a target. She had nearly crashed to her death mere hours earlier. But her mother's rejection had been the last straw, and Jack wanted to shelter her.

He wished he could protect her from any harm. Somehow, he must expose the killer, draw him into the open so he could be caught and stopped. Jack knew he would protect Megan with his life. Hers was precious to so many people. He had seen it in Amber and Tess, in Janet and Gary. She had even made a strong impression on his sister.

And him. Yes, her life was precious to him. Too precious for his comfort. She wasn't his future. She couldn't be. After his training, he could be assigned anywhere in the country, even the world.

But he could protect her for now. He could comfort

her for now. She needed a shoulder to cry on, and his were pretty broad.

"Is everything all right here?" A security guard stopped in front of Jack.

He nodded. "She just got some bad news."

Not raising her head, Megan nodded.

"Glad she's not alone then." The guard moved on to break up a shoving match among some teens.

"Being alone is the hardest thing," Jack said.

Megan nodded. "I knew they didn't want to see me until I came to my senses, of course. But this? I thought they would change their minds. I thought my own parents would protect me. I didn't want to go to them, but they didn't give me a chance." She raised her head and wiped her sleeve across her eyes. "I don't know why they still hurt me after all this time."

"Because they're your parents. They're supposed to stand up for you no matter what."

"Did yours? Stand up for you, that is?"

"They did. They didn't have any problem telling me when I was wrong, but they didn't punish me until they had the facts."

"You were blessed."

"I was. And so are you."

She frowned. "How?"

"Your parents are still alive. You still have time to mend your fences with them."

"They rejected me."

"Or did you reject them?" Jack risked touching her curls, brushing wayward strands behind her ears. "They planned a future that would leave you safe and secure."

"Not one I wanted. Not the one I felt I was called to do." She pushed herself away from him, hands on his chest. "But everyone always takes their side."

"I'm not taking their side." Jack covered her hands with his. "I'm just suggesting you look at things from their perspective. They don't think you were raised for the rough life of a PI."

"Yes, I'm a North Shore princess."

"I think you'd survive any revolt of your subjects."

Megan laughed and freed her hands. "Now I have to figure out where to go."

"To my aunt and uncle's. You know they'll have you."

"I don't want to be trouble."

"You'll be trouble if we're all worried about you." Jack hefted her duffel onto his shoulder and laced his fingers through hers. "Let's go. Rush hour is nearly over, and the trains will come slower than a deep-dish pizza."

"Oh, pizza." Megan drew tissues from her bag and mopped at her face. "I could use some."

"You just had some yesterday."

"And the problem with that is?" She smiled up at him, though tears still clung to her lashes.

Had they been alone, he would have kissed her again. A good thing they were moving through the lobby of a busy train station. He should not kiss her. He should not touch her at all.

He didn't let go of her hand. As long as he could hold onto her, he knew she was safe.

Back on the street, they walked fast and aware of their surroundings, of the people passing them in either direction. A mist rolled in from the lake, creating halos on the streetlights and turning people into mere shadows. Cars drove toward them like white-eyed monsters, then swooshed past on rain-wet streets. Swooshed, sped, crept past depending on the traffic patterns, until one car didn't continue in the flow of vehicles along Madison.

Jack never knew what alerted him. Maybe the glimpse

of a face through the windshield. Maybe a change in the engine. Whatever the signal, he knew that car wasn't going to continue with the flow of traffic.

"Megan," Jack said quietly. "Run."

She didn't hesitate. With a glance at the car, she took off, Jack with her, still holding her hand. They were together. They could survive if they stayed together.

No one could outrun a car. Their only advantage was their direction of egress. The car would have to turn.

Turn it did. No waiting for the corner to complete a U-turn. No driving around the block. The sedan gunned the engine to clear the curb and spun a 180 in the middle of the sidewalk.

People screamed and shouted and scattered into blackened doorways. These were businesses here and not shops and restaurants. These places were closed for the night. No way to duck inside the shelter of solid brick and mortar. Jack and Megan were on their own in the open.

They darted between cars in the street. A cacophony of horns followed them. One vehicle came close enough to Jack he felt the heat from its radiator. But they were on the other sidewalk, headed in the opposite direction of the errant car. A moment's reprieve.

Only a moment. Behind them, the car roared back into the street, once again headed in the same direction as Jack and Megan.

With tight maneuvers that probably took the paint off one or two cars, the pursuing vehicle cut across traffic and onto the opposite pavement. The engine roared, louder than the rest of the cars together. Drawing closer. Closer. Too close. The only thing slowing it were the throngs of people not yet out of its way. The driver couldn't mow down a dozen pedestrians and still reach Jack and Megan.

But people were scattering left and right, into doorways, into the street.

Jack and Megan dared not do the same. They needed more secure shelter. If they ceased, the driver could more easily shoot them. He hadn't proved to be a good shot so far, but that could change if they stopped moving.

Jack risked a glance back. The monster's eyes loomed like death beams. To their right, traffic flowed fast and thick, bumper to bumper, compacts interspersed with trucks and buses. Just as dangerous as the beast behind him and Megan. To their left, revolving doors and plate glass windows. If just one was open—

Megan tugged his hand and pointed. One was open ten feet ahead. Heads down, they sprinted toward it just as the car behind them stepped on the gas with the roar of a V-8 engine.

FIFTEEN

The headlights streamed past them, bright paths of danger on the night-dimmed sidewalk. The roar may as well have been a freight train ready to charge right over them. It filled Megan's ears, her heart, her every breath.

No, not breath. She couldn't breathe. Concrete had replaced her lungs. Each inhalation was an effort. Every muscle screamed in protest as more effort was demanded than it could provide. Still, Jack clutched her hand, drawing her forward, pressing on to greater speed.

Useless. They couldn't outrun a speeding car. Cars didn't speed on sidewalks, but this one did. She and Jack had been found. How. Why? No time to think of that now. Must run. Get away.

Mercifully no one else seemed to be in the way. Just her and Jack. Two flies about to find themselves flattened by tons of steel.

Unless they reached the revolving door spinning slowly ahead of them. Spinning into the glorious golden light of a lobby. Spinning into relative safety. A car could smash plate glass, damage bricks. Megan planned for her and Jack to be in the next street by that time.

They hit the revolving door together, both of them cramming into the wedge between panels together. When it spilled them on the other side, they didn't stop. A security guard shouted to them, but they kept running straight back, past the sign-in desk, past the elevator bank.

"Duck," Jack shouted to the guard.

Before Megan and Jack reached the doors on the other side of the building, a crash of breaking glass and the female guard's scream reverberated in the vaulted chamber. Megan and Jack didn't stop. They slammed through the opposite revolving door, across the street, and down the entrance to a subway train.

At the bottom of the steps, they stopped and leaned against the tiled wall, hands on knees, breathing like aged locomotives puffing steam.

"I don't think I can walk another step," Megan gasped in bursts. "Not…one…step."

Jack merely nodded as he let her duffel slide to the floor.

She stared at it. "You didn't drop that?"

"You need it."

"But the extra weight. It must have slowed you down."

She must have slowed him down.

She stared at him. "Were we really just chased by a car driving on the sidewalk?"

"We were." Jack brushed his coat sleeve across the beads of perspiration on his forehead.

"But they could have hurt so many people out there."

He adored her for thinking of others.

The wail of a siren kept him from responding.

Megan groaned. "Not again."

They started to laugh. The situation wasn't funny, but it called for laughter or tears, and they opted for the former. No one—surely no one—had ever filed so many police reports in so few days.

Until now.

Laughing left them breathless again and brought them a number of odd looks from passersby. They were a spectacle. They would be remembered.

"We'd better go up and take our medicine," Jack said.

"You make it sound like we're the bad guys."

"Filling out police reports makes me feel like a criminal." Jack hefted her duffel over his shoulder again and held out his hand.

She placed hers in it as though doing so were the most natural act in the world. It felt natural. Warm. Permanent.

Except it wasn't. He wasn't. A relationship with him certainly was not.

Walking up the steps to the street level looked as difficult as climbing Pike's Peak. The elevator was nowhere to be seen, so they began to climb, resting on the landing, and starting up again.

Flashing lights lit the sky above, a sea of emergency vehicles.

"Not our doing," Megan repeated. "I keep telling myself I'm not to blame."

Yet she felt responsible. She had climbed that tree to finish a case with haste. She was anxious for closed cases and more cases, wanting to be worthy of owning the agency.

"Don't blame yourself," Jack said. "This is the work of a greedy, immoral man and woman at the least."

"But I was greedy. If I hadn't been—"

"Hush." Jack laid a finger across her lips. "You were doing your job in the most ethical way you could. You aren't responsible for someone else's wrong choices."

They reached the sidewalk and began to loop around the now cordoned-off building. They could have gone to a police car on the back side of the building but chose to reach the front. By tacit consent, they agreed to see what had happened to the car and people inside before they found themselves tangled in hours of speaking to detectives.

From a block away, they witnessed the destruction the car had caused. The set of revolving doors and surrounding plate glass windows had been shattered into billions of shards of glass. Mortar and bricks lay on the sidewalk and crumpled hood of the car. Steam rose from the radiator, and two firemen hosed the engine down with foam, suggesting it had caught fire.

What they didn't see was anyone in custody. No cops held either a man or woman on the pavement, and not one cop car had passengers in the back.

The would-be killers had gotten away.

Megan sighed and squared her shoulders. Surely the killers left some clue behind with every attempt on their lives. Something would link them to the Cahill murder and several attempts to kill her and Jack.

She fished her PI credentials from her bag and made her way to a man who wore jeans and a sport coat but held himself like a police officer.

She took a deep breath and called to him. "Sir, I can tell you what happened here."

He faced her, scowling. "I can see what happened here. Move along."

"No, I mean I can tell you why this happened." She held up her PI license. "I'm Megan O'Clare, and the driver of that car was trying to kill us."

The rest of the night was as tedious as Jack feared. Questions. Written reports. More questions. A meal of fast food that filled his stomach and left him hollow.

Or maybe that was from something else. He'd been feeling hollow all day. Maybe since kissing Megan, one of the most foolish moves of his life. Maybe from simple fatigue and worry. Maybe he had been feeling hollow before he kissed Megan and that had driven him to making that poor decision.

Except the only error he truly believed he had made with Megan was startling her so she fell out of that tree.

That was a mistake toward her *and* a mistake toward him because he had come to like her too much.

He wished she had been able to go to her parents' place. A final goodbye would be good for both of them. Now they spent more hours together, talking, trying to find humor in their situation, holding hands because they needed an anchor in a world that was spinning out of control. And he didn't want to let her go.

So he should. He needed to figure out a way to draw out this killer when Megan wasn't with him. He could make himself a target. If he got her someplace safe, he could play killer bait.

By the time he reached his aunt and uncle's place, Dave was getting home. Aunt Julie made them a hearty breakfast before heading into her office for work. Grace appeared worried or in pain, with dark circles under her eyes and a down-droop to her lips.

"You've got to take care of yourself," she admonished him.

"I'm trying, sweetheart."

Not hard enough.

He studied her sweet, pretty face and thought about what would happen to her if anything happened to him. She would miss him, for sure. Yet these past few months had shown all of them how strong she was. She would continue to heal. Dave and Julie would take great care of her.

And Megan, practically falling asleep in her orange

juice, would miss him, too. That was all right. That was best. She would throw herself into her work and make a great success of the investigative agency. And she would be safe. They would all be safe.

He had to get her to safety first. Unlike Grace, she wouldn't remain with Dave and Julie if he wasn't there. Her parents' house had seemed like the best option. Yet they had said that they weren't there.

"Why don't you all get some sleep," Aunt Julie suggested, returning to the kitchen. "We'll all be quiet."

"Just a couple hours," Jack said. "Then we need to do some planning."

But sleep was so necessary to reacting well to danger. Fatigue dulled the senses, slowed reaction time.

"I can't see straight I'm so tired," Megan mumbled. She drained her orange juice and began to gather dishes.

"Leave those," Aunt Julie said. "I can get them."

"I can help." Grace used chair backs and the countertop to support herself on the way to the sink. Propped against the counter, she began to rinse dishes for the dishwasher.

She had begun doing this at home in the past few weeks. She needed to feel useful in any way she could, and Jack looked for tasks to keep her occupied, keep her motivated to get well.

Jack caught Megan gazing at Grace with such a look of tenderness his heart felt like it might melt from a flood of warmth inside him. Grace had been a great kid before her accident. Her injuries seemed to have brought out the best in her, and Megan seemed to recognize and admire his sister's strength.

"I should help," Megan said.

"You would probably fall asleep on your feet and drop a stack of plates," Jack told her.

She gave him a half smile. “I might.”

“Go to my room,” Grace said. “I got my stuff out of there.”

Megan smiled her thanks. “At least I have clean clothes with me this time.” Then she was gone down the hallway.

Assured Aunt Julie could work in the dining room so he could use her office to sleep, Jack made his own way along the hall. He barely remembered unfolding the sofa bed. He didn’t dream. He slept solid for three hours, then woke to the buzzing of his phone.

It was a text from Megan. When you’re ready, we need to figure out what to do next.

Finding clean clothes folded over a chair, Jack got ready and emerged into the living room, where Megan stood looking at the lake and sipping from a mug of coffee. By way of greeting, she pointed to a carafe and mug resting on a tray atop the coffee table. Once he held a cup of steaming coffee in hand, he joined her at the window.

“Get some sleep?” he asked.

“Yes. Not enough, but it helps.” She gestured outside. “It’s so clear today. That blue is incredible.”

“I expect I’ll miss it. The Chesapeake Bay isn’t quite the same.”

“It’s still beautiful, though.”

“You’ve seen it?”

She nodded. “I’ve seen most places in the US, and a few others.”

“I’ve hardly been anywhere.” He grinned. “When I was growing up, going to Wrigley Field was like traveling to a foreign country.”

She grinned back, then sobered. “What do we do now?”

“You leave town.” Jack had his speech prepared and held up a hand to stop her inevitable protest. “Do your parents have a vacation home somewhere? Or do you know a private resort you can get into? Because I was thinking about what your mother said. She didn't say she wouldn't help you. Surely she can provide you with the means to get someplace safe."

"With money. It's always money with them."

"But sometimes money comes in handy, like when you don't want to use a credit card."

Her eyes filled. "I want them for once to acknowledge me."

"Have you ever told them that, or just walked away and rejected them?"

"I—" She gulped, then ducked her head. "I rejected them. I never go back there."

"Do they invite you?"

She nodded. "I'm tired of being told what I want to do isn't good enough for them."

"I know. I was supposed to be a cop like my uncle and dad, and I failed at it. I suppose my uncle is accepting of me now because I got into the FBI Academy. But I'm going to pretend he cares about me regardless of what I do."

"He does. That's obvious. But it's different with my parents. They don't care about me unless I do what they want me to do."

"Are you sure? Have you given them a chance?"

"They'll never accept me being a PI. Maybe if I own the agency." She wrinkled her nose. "That would make me a businesswoman."

His heart softened for her. Her desperation to own the agency was to win over her family. He understood. His wish to join the FBI in the nonaction position of accountant just might be to please his family.

He shifted uncomfortably with the revelation and

snapped his focus back to Megan. "Will you ask your parents to help you find a place to hide out for a while?"

"I will. Maybe." She kept her gaze on the blue sky and bluer lake striped with the white lines of wave crests. "Probably." She fumbled at her jeans pocket and pulled out her phone. "A bank transfer would take too long, maybe even a whole day. But they have staff who could meet me somewhere. But what about you?"

"I'll do what I can to draw out this killer," he said aloud.

"Jack, no, that's too dangerous." Her eyes were huge in her pale face.

"I'll stay safe. I'm a little harder to kill than a small woman."

"You're still flesh and blood. I mean, they shot you once already." She moved toward him. "You should come with me."

"I'd like to. That would make me happier. But if we're apart, they'll have a harder time." He shrugged. "You know, divide and conquer."

"A house divided cannot stand," she shot back.

"But we're not against ourselves. We're united in our division. That is, our goal is united." She was close enough for him to brush his fingertips along her cheek. "You've been a great person to go through this with, if we had to go through it."

"You, too." Her voice was husky. She turned her head to kiss his fingertips, then scurried away. "I'll make that phone call and get my stuff."

Jack set his unfinished coffee on the tray and sought out his aunt.

He found her in her office, hooking up her computer to the power cord. "We're taking off."

"You're coming back, aren't you?" Her face and voice registered alarm.

"I should be. Megan is going to ask her parents for help finding a place to hide out until the killer is caught." Jack's throat felt tight.

Aunt Julie gazed at him thoughtfully for a moment, then asked, "You care about her, don't you?"

Jack inclined his head. "But there's no point in it. Her life is here, and mine will be in Virginia."

"She can't be a PI in Virginia?"

"I expect she can get a license there after a while, but she won't own the agency. She won't have the clientele she has here. It'll be starting all over."

"And she's not willing to do that for you?" She frowned. "Or didn't you ask?"

"Of course I didn't ask. I can't expect her to give up everything to follow me and take on Grace and me being gone for possibly weeks at a time and—" He sighed. "It's too much to ask of her, especially if she is able to start repairing some of the hurt with her family."

"So you don't think she'd say yes?" Aunt Julie pressed.

"I'm not going to put her into that dilemma. We just don't know one another well enough."

Yet he felt like he had known her forever.

"Maybe if we had more time before I leave..." He shifted his shoulders, trying to alleviate a heaviness settling over him. "But that's a moot point now. Right now, I just want to get that killer caught so Megan has a future and the people I love aren't at risk."

He wouldn't mention himself being at risk. Aunt Julie would find a way to stop him.

"I'm ready to go." Megan knocked on the door. "Thank you for everything, Mrs. Luskie."

Aunt Julie rose and hugged Megan. "Happy to do what I can. You take care of yourself."

"You're coming back, aren't you?" Grace emerged into the hallway.

Megan faced her. "I don't think so, but I'm so glad I met you. If you want to be a PI, come look me up."

Grace laughed. "I want to be a lawyer."

"Maybe my mother should adopt you." Megan hugged Grace, picked up her duffel and headed toward the door.

Jack followed. He didn't say goodbye to Grace. She would sense he was up to something. She knew him too well.

Though he and Megan walked side by side to the elevator, they didn't speak until they were across the lobby, where Jack paused just inside the glass doors. "We have what I hope is unobtrusive police escort to the nearest L station, thanks to my uncle. They should make sure we're not followed this time."

"I hope so," Megan said.

Then they fell silent all the way to the nearest L station, this one actually underground, they didn't speak until they were belowground. Post rush hour, the crowds were light, the trains less frequent. They stood in an isolated pocket outside the turnstiles and still took several moments to speak. When they did, they spoke at once.

"You talked to your parents?" Jack asked.

"My father. My mother was on a conference call." She took a deep breath. "I'm meeting one of their staff halfway between here and North Point. They'll have money and a car for me."

"And you won't say where?"

"I'd better not." Her smile was wan. "And I don't know where I'm going. Probably Wisconsin or—"

He laid a finger across her lips. "Don't say where even to me."

"Right." She ran her tongue over her lower lip after he moved his hand away. "You be careful," Megan said.

"Take care of yourself," Jack said.

They smiled.

"I'm so glad I met you," Jack said.

"Me, too. I mean, I'm glad I met you." Megan hefted her duffel higher onto her shoulder. "You be careful at the academy. I hear the training is rough. And Grace needs you."

"Don't let being the boss go to your head." He meant to simply chuck her under the chin like a mere companion, yet once his knuckles made light contact, he let his fingers linger, tilting up her face to his. "Take care," he whispered, then he kissed her.

"Thanks," she murmured, then spun on her heel and shoved through the turnstile.

Jack followed. He saw her on the platform below and took the steps that led to the opposite platform. For several minutes, they stood across from one another, the tracks and high voltage rails a gulf between them. His heart ached, and he knew he was making a terrible mistake. He needed to stop this, stop her, stop himself. He couldn't let her go, never see her again.

"Megan," he called.

No way could she hear him. The platform had begun to vibrate with the rumble of the oncoming train. In the closed tunnel, the approaching subway roared like a beast seeking its next meal. A meal of passengers it would gather in, then disgorge further down the track. This one was going to swallow Megan. It swooped into the station, blocking her from view.

And Jack heard her scream.

He started to run, knowing he didn't have enough time to race up one flight and down another. He knew she couldn't hear him, but he shouted her name again and again.

He reached the mezzanine above the tracks just as the train on the opposite side pulled away from the station—pulled away without Megan aboard, for her duffel lay abandoned on the platform like a crumpled messenger.

SIXTEEN

Jack rested one hand against a round, tiled pillar and scanned the station. The line of passengers was mostly disbursed. Jack feared that the thinning of the crowd had less to do with his villain than the time of day. If Megan had emitted more than that cry of fear, not many would hear her. Fewer were likely to respond. Yet someone might have seen her.

He glanced around for the customer service agent, for one of the people with nothing much to do but ride around on the trains all day, for a custodian. Below, he saw a customer service agent emerge onto the platform and pick up the duffel. She would probably carry it off to lost and found and no sign Megan had been there would remain.

He leaned over the railing. "'Scuse me, miss?"

She glanced up, blue-dyed hair falling away from an unnaturally white face. "Yeah?"

"I'm looking for someone. A small woman with red hair. That's her duffel." He felt a little sick at that. "Have you seen her?"

The woman shook her head.

Security cameras. Surely they had security cameras. But a CSA wouldn't have access to those. No one would give him access to a video feed for security. But it might show something.

It would take hours to find out. But he doubted he had hours.

"Is anyone else working the station today?" he asked.

The CSA pointed to the booth.

Jack thanked her out of curtesy more than because she'd been helpful, and she took Megan's duffel to the booth for safekeeping. The agent would send it to the lost and found center, and Jack's hands would be unencumbered.

He slipped through the turnstile. A woman sat in the booth eating take-out Chinese food. When he knocked on the window, she shook her head. She wasn't interrupting her meal to answer his question.

"Please," he called through the glass. "It's an emergency."

She pointed behind him. Figuring he meant the other CSA was coming, he persisted. "She hasn't seen my friend, and I think she's in danger."

For response, the woman stood and drew down a shade to cover the window.

Teeth gritted, Jack stomped away and approached a woman with a handful of invitations to her church. "Excuse me, ma'am, have you seen a small woman with curly red hair go past here?" He gulped down a lump of anxiety rising in his throat and added the detail he didn't want to think about. "She might have been with a big man with heavy brows."

Even before he finished his queries, the woman was shaking her head. "But please take this pamphlet." She thrust it into his hand.

He shoved it into his pocket and stalked away, seeking someone else to ask. Surely more people needed to ride a train even that late in the evening. People worked late. People worked odd hours. People went out to dinner.

He paused at the turnstiles again and was wondering if he should slide his card and go back inside, when someone tapped him on the shoulder.

"I've seen her." The voice was low, husky and female.

Jack turned slowly so as not to startle her. He expected another passenger, a tired-looking career woman coming home from working late. Instead, he saw the woman, the one he and Megan had mistaken for Cahill from a distance. Both were tall and willowy. Both had long blond hair. And both had noses with a decided bump like a ski jump just below the bridge. Resemblances ended there. Cahill's face had been sweet. This woman's face was hard.

So was the barrel of the gun she pressed into his abdomen under the cover of an oversize handbag hanging from one shoulder, and a computer case from the other.

"Be quiet and you can live long enough to see her again."

"You won't shoot me in here. It's a public place." His words held more certainty than he felt.

He thought she might risk it. The tiled and vaulted ceiling would mask the true location of the shots. By the time anyone figured out the direction, the woman would be gone, and Jack would be as good as dead.

And he knew that, more than anything, he wanted to live long enough to see Megan again.

He never should have said goodbye to her. But he had, and there he was being guided away by threat of death, onto an elevator that emptied into the middle of a sidewalk. It too was deserted. Even the side street she led him down bore no cars other than those parked against the curb. Those were all dark, quiet and empty save for one tucked in the middle of the pack. It idled with the headlights off. Enough light from the streetlights showed the shadows of two people, one at the wheel and another one in the back seat. Light shone off the smaller person's hair, a mere two or three square inches of exposure, but Jack knew it was Megan.

Suddenly, he couldn't breathe. His heart beat too fast, too hard. He forced air into his lungs, drew a long, slow breath through his nose to calm himself. Now was not the time to act. He needed to spend time with these people, watch them in action to guess how they operated together and separately.

If he and Megan had enough time for observation.

"Get in." The woman poked him with the gun.

"You're going to let me sit in the back with Megan and not tie me?"

"Plan to outrun a bullet, do you?" The woman smiled and was rather terrifyingly pretty when she did so.

"Guess not." Jack smiled, too, then opened the car door and slid in beside Megan.

She wasn't going to be outrunning any bullets, either. The man in the front sat sideways as though he merely engaged her in conversation around the high back of his seat. But on the console between the front seats, he held a pistol trained on Megan's middle.

Smart, going after the middle like that. Hit the aorta and a body was dead before an ambulance could arrive. And the aorta was a huge artery, too easy to hit. And plowing a bullet through the liver, an even bigger target, didn't do a body much good, either. Center mass was easy to hit and most often led to a pretty quick death.

They didn't need ropes to bind them, ropes that were hard to explain after bodies were found. Bodies in accidents didn't wear ropes or have rope burns on their bodies.

Jack grasped Megan's hand. She clung to his fingers, hers freezing but steady and strong.

"That's my girl," he murmured.

The woman rounded the car and slid into the front passenger seat. The click of the child locks engaging preceded the driver turning the key in the lock and starting the engine.

This was an electric car, nearly silent gliding through the streets. Without lights, few people would even notice it had passed. No one would miss him and Megan. No one was expecting them.

They drove in silence until they reached Lake Shore Drive. Once they sped along the lake, Jack spoke. "Do you two have names? I mean, it's not like we can tell anyone who you are once you off us."

The man chuckled.

"Cahill," the woman said. "I'm Mary Cahill."

"Cahill." The name burst from Megan. "You're Cahill's sister?"

"Cousin. We have the family nose."

"So look alike from a distance," Megan said.

No wonder they had been confused when they saw her on the street that first night.

"And your buddy there with the Cro-Magnon brow?" Jack asked.

The man grunted.

"Blake Davis," Cahill supplied.

"Yeah, right." Jack snorted.

The name sounded like a movie star, not a criminal.

"So where are we going?" Megan stared out her windows at the city speeding past, lights flashing from buildings as they passed. "I don't recognize this side of town."

"I do." Jack squeezed her hand. "We're on the southside. Never been here before?"

She shook her head.

"You were told it's too dangerous, right?" Jack asked.

She nodded.

"Some of it is, but mostly it's just people trying to live their lives."

He hoped she got the message—that they would work to keep living their lives.

Even if she didn't understand his cryptic words, he never doubted she would work hard to keep them both alive.

"It's dangerous enough." Cahill snickered. "Or will be for you."

"You had no business watching us," Davis blurted.

"I'm a PI," Megan said. "Of course I did. More business than you killing Ms. Cahill."

"She wanted to keep too big a share of the money," Davis said.

"Of course." Jack looked into the rearview mirror and curled his upper lip. "Money. What else?"

"She had plenty already and wanted to keep our share," Cahill, the cousin, said.

"But didn't she embezzle it?" Jack asked.

"Sure, but we were going to get her away safe out of the country," Davis said.

"So you killed her." Jack shook his head as though he pitied the two culprits in the front. "You should have taken off then and there."

"And leave witnesses?" Mary Cahill grimaced. "We couldn't leave you two loose ends."

"Loose cannons," the man grumbled.

"So now you have us and plan to do what with us?" Jack asked with all the skill he possessed to maintain a mild manner.

Beside him, Megan shuddered.

"We're not going to tell you and let you think you can stop us," Davis said.

Not so dumb after all.

They all fell silent after that. Davis left Lake Shore Drive and began wending his way through streets seemingly at random. After a while, Jack figured out he was moving at random as if he thought he could confound them as to their destination. But Jack knew the city too well for that. He realized they moved through the part of the city that ran along the south side of Lake Michigan, stretching toward Indiana. With each zigzag pattern of the car, they moved closer to the lake. That lake and its numerous aging piers jutting over the water. The water was pretty polluted there from past and current industry. Yet people fished off the piers. Jack had fished off that pier with his father. They never kept anything they caught. They just liked the quiet time together.

Maybe someone would be fishing there that night. Not that anyone fishing on the pier on a cold night would do much to help. Long ago, the old men, most of them homeless, had learned to see nothing that went on around the southside piers. Too many bodies that disappeared beyond the water reclamation plants offshore, where the lake was deeper than anyone wanted to dive in water colder than a refrigerator, had begun their journey in a boat moored at one of the piers.

Not good. Very much not good.

He wanted to warn Megan so she could take an opportunity to get away if it offered itself. No, not offered itself. They would have to make one. But he dared not say anything and alert their captors they knew what was going on. Though their goal was mutual—staying alive—Megan and he had to work on their own and help one another if they could.

Davis stopped the car, and Jack's senses went on high alert. He must be aware of each sight, sound and touch around him. Anything could be a weapon. A piece of paper. A loose nail.

Davis and Cahill opened their doors. The child locks popped. Neither Megan nor Jack moved. Not with guns trained on them. Unless they could divert those guns from their persons, they needed to act meek and obedient.

But not too much so. Too much meekness could be just as suspicious as outright rebellion.

Jack gave Megan's hand one last squeeze and swung his legs from the car. "Let me guess, a long walk off a short pier."

"Ha ha. That was so funny I forgot to laugh." Davis laughed anyway. "But I will when you two are no longer a nuisance."

"Yeah, sure."

The gun poked Jack in the spine. He headed for the pier, dimly lit after dark. The sky was clear, but without a moon. A low-lying glow at the end of the pier suggested someone did fish there, a lantern beside him.

A lantern. A potential weapon.

Cahill and Megan started out first. Their footfalls rang in hollow thuds on the wooden planks. The light at the end swayed. The pier was ancient, wobbly. An advantage.

Jack followed six feet behind Megan and Cahill. The barrel of the pistol ground into his spine. The pain annoyed him mostly because he figured Megan was getting the same treatment and he didn't want her to suffer. If he couldn't save her, at least he hoped she wouldn't suffer.

He kept his gaze on that lantern, on the man who studiously kept his back to them. The man would never see a thing. He could be questioned for hours and be able to claim he never saw a thing.

Weapon. Distraction. Fuel. He needed fuel for his weapon, a way to arm it.

He set his hands on his hips as though he were too cool to care he was on his way to being executed—and felt the crackle of paper in his pocket. The brochure from the lady at the subway station. Jack made his first move, a simple trip over a loose board. Davis growled something and yanked him upright. A precedent was set. Another yard, two, three.

Jack stumbled again, caught hold of a mooring post for balance, and kicked over the lantern. The glass chimney broke. Oil and a tiny flame poured onto the pier. Jack dropped the brochure into the fuel as a little easier kindling than the waterlogged pier.

"What did you do?" Davis shouted.

Cahill spun, gun momentarily off Megan's back.

And Megan dove off the pier and into the frigid water of Lake Michigan.

Water closed over Megan's head oily and foul and the best thing she'd felt since Jack let go of her hand. Better at that moment because it meant freedom, potential rescue.

She had plunged between two moored boats. Not much protection, especially when Davis began to fire into the water. One bullet smacked the surface less than a foot from Megan's head. Holding her nose against the stench of the water, she drew in a lungful of air and dove. She had no idea how deep bullets could penetrate. She needed to be out of range, needed a shield.

She dove under the pier. Slimy pilings slithered past her. She shuddered from more than the cold. And the cold was bad enough. If she remained in the water too long, she would contract hypothermia and be no good to Jack, let alone herself. The killers wouldn't need to murder her. The water would do it for them.

Or maybe they planned that all along. Dump their bodies where the lake grew deep. Even if they were recovered, they would have no rope marks or wounds on their persons.

If she stayed in the water much longer, she would be sick. She would also be of no use to Jack.

She continued beneath the pier, listening hard for what might be going on above. Shouting. Davis shouting at Cahill. She was stupid for letting Megan go. She'd better find her.

Glad the pier wasn't very wide, Megan emerged on the other side. So far, no one had come to look for her there. She grasped the gunwale of a boat and hoisted herself up. If she kicked, she could get herself inside the craft and seek a weapon. If she kicked, she would draw attention to herself. If she drew attention to herself, Jack had a chance to get away.

Sadly, she smelled no smoke. Davis or Cahill or even the fisherman must have put out the fire. Clever Jack for starting it, though. She was free. If she could get into the boat.

She risked a strong enough kick to propel herself over the gunwale and into the boat. It wasn't much, merely a fiberglass fishing boat, big enough to be lake-worthy and small enough to be easy to maneuver. Maybe it had a blanket she could exchange for her soaked coat.

On her knees in the bottom of the craft for a low profile, she looked over the edge of the pier. Davis stomped along the edge of the pier, staring down. Looking for her. Cahill held her gun on Jack. The fisherman had vanished. Megan didn't dare hope he would go for help. He was more likely to disappear into a distant alleyway. At the moment, she saw no way for Jack to escape. Too soon, Davis would begin searching for her on this side of the pier.

She turned her attention to the boat, seeking a locker with a blanket, a life jacket, an emergency supply kit.

Emergency supplies.

Careless of noise, she sought more frantically, tossing fishing gear into the bottom of the boat, a thermos, a number of unidentifiable objects. No blanket. No life jacket.

But an emergency kit.

A shout yanked her attention back to the pier. Jack had turned sideways to Cahill and looked about to dive into the lake. Cahill raised her gun hand, squeezed off a round.

Megan crammed her arm between her teeth to stop herself from screaming, sure Jack would be shot at that close a range.

But he didn't fall. He ducked and shoved his shoulder into the woman's solar plexus. Her gun fired again, the bullet slamming into the pier. She shrieked as Jack hoisted her over his shoulder and toward the edge of the pier until she was screaming longer and louder as she tumbled into the water to land with a splash.

This time, Jack tried to follow. He didn't make it. Davis had his left arm around Jack's neck and his gun against Jack's temple.

"If you can hear me, Miss Megan O'Clare," Davis said, "get back here or he's dead."

Megan didn't move. She knew Jack would want her to save herself, and she knew she couldn't leave him there to die while she went free. She wanted to stay with him, keep trying to rescue him, as long as she was allowed. Stay with him forever no matter what.

"Don't listen to him, Megan," Jack called.

"To the count of ten," Davis said.

Helped by the splashing from the other side of the pier, Megan tore into the emergency kit as quietly as she could. Everything she needed was there.

"Five, four, three," Davis was counting.

"Two, one," Megan mouthed with him—and struck the match.

With a crackling whoosh, the red flare arced into the sky. Too high. Too high. Too high. But a distraction nonetheless.

Still holding Jack, Davis spun toward Megan. She ducked and prepared a second flare. She only had it and one more. It needed to count. She threw it this time, tossed it into a boat two moorings away. Fiberglass wouldn't burn, but boats always had fuel spilled somewhere.

This one did. It lit like an Independence Day celebration, a bottle rocket gone wild. The percussion and heat knocked Megan backward. But she'd remembered to close her eyes.

Final flare in hand, she opened her eyes and scrambled onto the pier, half expecting to be shot on sight. Light from the burning boat lit the stage of the pier like floodlights. Lit it enough to show Jack and Davis fighting, Jack taller and faster, Davis burlier and meaner. Jack's right arm wasn't working right. His wound from the other night. It must have opened again, weakening him. If Davis knocked him down, he could go for his gun. It lay on the planks like a snake ready to bite.

Megan crept forward, aware of punching fists and kicking feet. Davis wore boots. Jack wore running shoes. The latter were nearly useless for subduing an enemy. Blows from the boots made Jack wince. He favored his left leg already.

Megan stopped creeping and lunged for the gun. Her fingers closed over the barrel.

Davis snatched it from her hand, pointed it at her middle.

Megan held the match toward the last flare.

"Drop the flare," Davis commanded.

"Drop the gun." Megan made herself smile.

"I can't swim," Cahill shouted from the water.

"I can kill you before you can set that off," Davis said.

Megan shrugged. "Willing to risk being wrong?"

From the corner of her eye, she saw a shadow moving, Jack's shadow ducking behind the row of stations in the middle of the pier. If she could keep Davis's attention…

She scraped the match on a mooring post to light it. "You saw what that flare did to that boat over there. What do you think one would do to you?"

"A bullet will mess up your pretty face for an open casket."

Megan laughed. "Who's going to find my body but a few thousand fish?" She held the match perilously close to the flare.

Davis's eyes widened.

"Desperate times and all that," Megan said.

Jack was nearly behind Davis, reaching out.

Davis must have sensed the movement, heard a footfall. He spun the gun toward Jack.

Megan sent the third flare into the pier a foot behind Davis's feet. He yelled and jumped. Jack chopped the side of his hand into Davis's forearm, and the gun dropped.

This time Megan got it into her hand, muzzle pointed at Cahill's killer. The flare fizzled out on the wet planks of the pier. And in the near distance, sirens began to wail. The burning boat had done more than distract a killer—the flames had attracted law enforcement.

SEVENTEEN

Megan woke in a hospital bed with her mother seated beside her. She blinked against the sunlight flooding the room, closed her eyes and opened them again.

Her mother was still there.

"How?" was all she managed.

"Your former boss called me." Mother's voice, like her appearance, was perfectly modulated. Every hair was in place. She wore diamond earrings and pearls around her neck over a powder blue sweater. Her hair had once been red like Megan's but was now carefully dyed blond. "He thought I might like to know what you've been through because I was so callous as to not let you come stay with us."

"He would defend— Wait!" Megan sat up, wondering with a corner of her mind why she was in a hospital bed. "You said *former boss*. Did he fire me?"

"No, he apparently turned the agency over to you, so you're the boss now." A mild shudder was all the emotion she showed.

"But I don't have the money yet."

"He said he knows you're good for it." Mother smoothed her black pencil skirt with French-tipped fingers. "But I apparently have a choice between a daughter who is a private investigator and not having a daughter at all." Her lower lip gave the tiniest of quivers. "Apparently I came too close to not having a daughter at all."

Megan held out her hand. "You've always had a daughter. Please forgive me for not being a better one."

"I guess you can't deny your calling." Mother took her hand.

They sat like that for several minutes. Then her father slipped into the room, dressed in his white coat. A stethoscope dangled from his pocket, and for a moment, Megan thought he was going to take her vitals. He simply took her other hand, careful not to dislodge the IV sticking out of her wrist, and the three of them remained in silent understanding until a nurse did arrive to take Megan's vitals.

"You're doing pretty well considering," the nurse said. "Maybe another day here."

"Why am I here at all?" Megan asked.

"You passed out," Father said. "Seems your swim left you a little too cold to manage after too many days without enough sleep and a number of harrowing experiences." He gave her a stern look. "Don't do it again."

"It shouldn't have happened this time. Most PI work is routine, not dangerous."

One question burned on her lips, but she didn't know if she dared ask them. They might not even know. She wasn't sure she wanted to know if the answer was the wrong one.

So she asked the second most important question. "What happened to Cahill and Davis?"

"Who?" Mother asked.

"The killers," Megan said.

Mother didn't try to subdue her shudder this time.

"Locked up," Father said. He pulled up a chair. "How

did you manage to get yourself caught? We offered to help you get to safety."

"I—" Megan ducked her head. "I heard your message and only heard you say I wasn't welcome. So I…kept running. Then—then—" Her cheeks heated. "Then Jack pointed out what I'd been too upset to catch, so I was on my way to Mother's office to ask for help getting away for a while."

"But you were on the train," Mother said. "Why not a taxi?"

"I thought a taxi could be followed. We thought we evaded any followers on the way to the L. And then we changed trains and… We weren't clever enough."

"You were clever enough to get away." Father patted her hand and released it. "I guess all those summer camps taught you something."

"I would rather have gone out on boats with you," Megan dared.

"Yes, well—" Father cleared his throat. "Maybe when I retire, if your mother hasn't decided to run for president by then."

Mother gave out her modulated laugh. "I'll settle for mayor of a small town. It has enough stresses to manage."

"And I'll still be here," Megan said.

And Jack would be in Virginia.

She especially couldn't leave now that Gary had entrusted the agency to her.

They sat in silence for several more minutes, then Father cleared his throat and asked, "Who is Jack?"

The man I love.

"My friend," Megan said.

"Friend?" Mother raised her brows a millimeter. "I thought from the way he was worrying about you he was much more."

Megan shook her head. "He's going into the FBI in a few months."

"And we thought you being a PI was bad."

Jack was dismissed. Her parents remained for another half hour, then had to go prepare for some fundraiser dinner. They talked of inconsequential matters except for an invitation to Thanksgiving dinner.

"I will be there," Megan promised.

Each kissed her on the forehead before departing. A few minutes later, Mel, Gary and Janet arrived. That was a far more comfortable and far less important session of talking over the case and the agency and what came next.

Megan pretended to be ecstatic over gaining the agency. She knew she should be. It was all she had wanted for years. Now the victory felt hollow, her future lonely.

But Jack wasn't around. She was glad. She was vain enough to not want him to see her with her hair nasty from its dive into the lake and with her wearing pajamas with tigers on them, a gift from Mel. She at least wanted clean hair and real clothes when she saw him. If she saw him.

She was glad to be alone after her afternoon of company. She needed sleep. The hospital wouldn't have been her top choice of places to get sleep, but it worked. She slept through staff talking and patients demanding care. She barely woke to have her vitals taken in the morning and see the doctor who pronounced her fit and able to go home.

She didn't know how she was getting there, but her mother's personal assistant arrived with a pile of gifts Megan knew would hold clothes too fancy for her lifestyle. She would rather have had her mother there but accepted the gifts as her mother's way of expressing her caring. Few things changed overnight, but the barriers had been breached and the healing begun.

And Megan looked through the parcels anyway once home. One held a black cashmere sweater she couldn't resist because it was so soft and warm. With her own jeans, she didn't feel overdressed at all. Hot chocolate in hand, she snuggled before the gas fireplace and wished Amber and Tess were there for company.

No, she wished Jack was there for company. She had no way to contact him or him her. Their phones were gone. No one could contact her.

Unless they just stopped by. She half expected someone to do so, Mel at the least. So she wasn't surprised when the intercom buzzed. Extra cautious now, she asked who wanted in instead of just releasing the door.

"It's Jack."

Her insides felt as though her cocoa had melted them. Or maybe it was the sound of his voice.

She released the door lock and waited. She wasn't proud. She stood in her doorway, listening to his footfalls on the steps. Fast footfalls as though he took them two at a time while running.

When he reached the top of the steps, he hesitated a moment, holding her gaze, then he took one stride forward and wrapped his arms around her. "You are the smartest, bravest, most beautiful—" His voice broke and he rested his cheek on the top of her head. "Oh, Megan, I love you so much."

"I love you, too." She tilted her head back and gazed into eyes as blue as the lake. "I know you're leaving, and this is stupid of us, but I can't help it. I love you—"

"Hush," he said.

Then he kissed her.

"Well, now." She grinned at him. "You'd better have honorable intentions after that."

"The most honorable." He released her and clasped her

hands. "I can't go down on one knee. Davis left me with some stiff muscles that make kneeling kinda painful. But my heart kneels before you now with me asking, Megan, will you marry me?"

"I… Jack, I…" Her heart plummeted under the gravity of reality. "I can't go to Virginia. Gary trusts me to run the agency."

"I know. I was thinking. I only wanted into the academy because I thought my aunt and uncle would approve of me more and I could make Grace proud to have me as a brother who was more than a failed city cop and boring accountant. But I realized that they love me as I am already, and I don't need to be anything but me to be loved."

"I'd rather you are just you and not a super cop with numbers." Megan gripped his hands. "So you're staying here?"

"If you'll have me and my sister, too, of course. She comes along with the deal. But mostly you get my heart."

"And you get my snooty family."

"I thought they were nice."

She took a step back. "You met them?"

"Of course. I had to ask for your father's permiss—"

"You didn't."

He laughed. "I did. Just to make him happy. It seemed like the right thing to do."

"As right as spending your future with me." It was a statement, not a question.

And with those words, Megan rose on her tiptoes, wrapped her arms around his neck and kissed him with all the promise of their future together.

* * * * *

If you enjoyed this story, don't miss
Laurie Alice Eakes's next romantic suspense,
available next year from Love Inspired Suspense!

Find more great reads at www.LoveInspired.com

Dear Reader,

Thank you for purchasing *Exposing a Killer*. Unlike other books I've written, this book is set primarily in Chicago. Looking back a couple of years, I can see where the seeds of this story began—with an experience that triggered a scene. I was looking for a shortcut between the L station and my house, when I discovered a warren of little streets and alleys. My imagination took over, and I pictured a chase scene through those narrow thoroughfares. The more I thought about it, the more fun I had picturing all the ways I could endanger my hero and heroine within a city. Instead of man against nature, I had man against manmade. Add this with a class I took on being a private investigator, and—voilà! A book set in concrete rather than country roads had begun.

Chicago has been my home for four years, and long before that, it was one of my favorite cities to visit. One of the city's best features is Lake Michigan. I tend to gush about it. When I was growing up in Michigan, I spent at least part of every summer on the lake, baking in the sun and dreaming of the stories I would one day write.

To learn more about my books, you can find me online at http://www.lauriealiceeakes.com.

Laurie Alice Eakes

COMING NEXT MONTH FROM
Love Inspired Suspense

DEADLY CARGO
Alaska K-9 Unit • by Jodie Bailey

Assigned to bring down a drug-smuggling ring, Alaska State Trooper Will Stryker and his K-9 partner must team up with bush pilot Jasmine Jefferson. But when someone tries to kill them, Will learns Jasmine has been living in witness protection. Are the attacks related to the case...or is someone out for revenge?

UNDERCOVER PROTECTION
by Maggie K. Black

When criminals invade Leia Dukes's family farmhouse to capture her and destroy evidence of old crimes, she's rescued by Jay Brock—the farmhand who broke her heart. To regain her trust, Jay reveals his secret: he's an undercover police officer hunting a serial killer. And only he can keep her alive.

DANGEROUS AMISH SHOWDOWN
by Mary Alford

Determined to protect the young witness in his care, US marshal Mason Shetler brings her to the Amish community he left behind. With his partner injured and their car totaled, Mason must hide them in the nearest shelter—the home of his childhood friend Willa Lambright. Under siege by ruthless criminals, can they all survive?

COLD CASE DOUBLE CROSS
Cold Case Investigators • by Jessica R. Patch

Convinced his brother was wrongly convicted of murder, detective Cash Ryland plans to find the real killer—even if it puts him in the line of fire. But he needs help from cold-case investigator Mae Vogel, whom he mistreated in high school. Together, they might just solve the murder...if the killer doesn't silence them first.

ATTEMPTED ABDUCTION
by Sommer Smith

After someone tries to abduct a baby from the NICU and the infant's mother disappears, nurse Lauren Beck must go into hiding with US marshal Grayson Thorpe to shield the little girl. But can they keep the baby out of the hands of a vicious gang?

RESCUE ON THE RUN
by Jaycee Bullard

After stumbling onto a bank robbery, Sheriff Cal Stanek and paramedic Abby Marshall are taken hostage. But their biggest concern is the third hostage—a pregnant teller in labor. Escape is essential, especially when they learn the robbery is a cover for a kidnapping...and only they can save the newborn.
